Convergence

Marion,
*   May all your convergences*
be happy ones!

Deborah Madar

Deborah Madar

NFB
<<<>>>
Buffalo, NY

D1260416

ISBN: 978-0692253137

Printed in the United States of America.

Madar, Deborah. Convergence/ 1ˢᵗ Edition

Grateful permission is made to the following for permission to reprint previously published material.

Abrams, General Creighton. "Letter to Returnees." <u>Tour 365</u> Spring-Summer Edition, 1970: p.1.

PIGFOOT MUSIC: Excerpt from "Darkness, Darkness," words and music by Jesse Colin Young. Copyright 1969 by RCA. Reprinted by permission of Jesse Colin Young (ASCAP).

WIXEN MUSIC PUBLISHERS, INC: Excerpt from "One Good Man," words and music by Janis Joplin. Copyright 1969 by Strong Arm Music. Reprinted by permission

NFB
119 Dorchester Road
Buffalo, NY 14213

For more information visit
Nofrillsbuffalo.com

Dedication

To my husband Gary Madar, who read and reread, listened, and then listened some more. All my love and gratitude.

To my screenwriter son, Jesse Stratton, for your brilliance and honesty.

To the rest of my "Beta Team": Anne-Marie Ray, Kathy Holser, Jane Murphy, Susan Penn, and Buddy Pace for your close reading and guidance.

To Retired Captain Lee Davies of the Jamestown Police Department for his insights.

To Kathy Holser, my friend since 7th grade, for her beautiful cover design.

To my amazing children: Jesse Stratton, Amanda Reszkowski, Randall Stratton, and Matthew Madar and their spouses and significants: Kellie, Dave, Ann, and Ryan, for your love and support. And to the bright lights they have brought forth who illuminate my path: Miles, Fiona, George, Daphne, and Lillian.

Contents

Convergence

<<◇>>

Chapter One — The Porch

Four decades earlier, he had tried to stand his ground on the porch of her childhood home. He had stared up into the cold, blue eyes of the girl's father and asserted his claim on her. The man treasured his daughter, and through this lens of love, the boy's unworthiness was magnified. The father had protected her from harm as best he could, except from her mother's wrath, for eighteen years. Now, this interloper with shoulder- length hair had ridden his piece-of-shit Super 90 motorcycle to their Catskill home, uninvited. He had planted a foot on the threshold of their lives for the past day and night and now he was refusing to leave.

"I have known people, students, who have done this successfully, Mr. Fray. They marry, they get an apartment, and finish college *together*." He was trying his best to use a reasonable tone. The last thing he wanted to do this morning was come off as cocky, as he had been told by friends and enemies alike, that he could be. He knew that he seemed more confident than most twenty year olds, but almost all of his peers had fathers in their lives. He had had to become a man without a father's guidance.

Mr. Fray glared at him and said nothing. He was due at the plant, where he was a shift supervisor, in the next half-hour. He had to drop his wife off at her job in the technical school cafeteria first. This kid was holding up the morning routine, just as he had interrupted the flow of their lives in many other ways over the past two days.

The boy tried to stay calm in spite of her father's glowering, to choke down the rising anxiety her absence from the porch was causing. "We can both keep our work-study jobs," he continued, "and I have a buddy who can get me in at the Dunkirk Ice Cream plant. I may be able to pick up a part-time night shift during the semester, and then I could go full time this summer."

Where *was* she? From the time he had woken up in her den, long legs draped over the arm of the tiny love seat where he had slept, he had expected her to come down from her bedroom, to greet him with a kiss, to assure him that everything would be fine. He watched as her father shook his head.

"She's not ready for marriage." The man's matter-of-fact tone made the boy feel more desperate.

"How can you know that?" His voice registered a half an octave higher than normal. It was a cool April morning, but the boy was sweating.

"I know it because she's inside, in her bedroom, waiting for you to be gone."

With a sudden move forward, the boy attempted to push past the burly man, tried to use momentum to make up for their unevenly matched bodies. As he strained toward the front door of her house, the flash of the drape on the picture window as it was pushed aside caught his eye. He *knew* she couldn't have agreed to the old man kicking him out. He expected to see her pretty face looking back at him, blue eyes opened wide in astonishment at her father's presumption. He took a step toward the window. But it was her ten- year-old brother who witnessed the shove that sent him tripping and sprawling down her porch steps.

The boy landed on his hands and knees at the bottom. He pushed himself up to stand, his arms at his sides, his palms bleeding and his ego bruised. The old man's Harley was parked next to his Honda. Wobbly and a bit off balance still, he angrily thrust his left foot forward in a kind of clumsy karate move, intending to kick the heavy machine over, but he left only a dusty boot mark on the polished chrome. He pulled his helmet on, and got on his bike. As he pulled away, he watched in his rearview mirror as her old man stood on the porch and calmly lit a cigarette.

The most miserable days of the boy's life followed on his return home. Although his mother, in anticipation of his break from school, had stocked the pantry with all his favorites and cooked delicious meals for him when she got home from work, he ate almost nothing. Each night, he pushed the food around on his plate, avoiding his mother's eyes. Friends from high school called and wanted him to go out to the bars, but he did not have the energy to pretend that he was fine.

During the week that remained of Spring Break, he tried daily to reach the girl, but she did not answer his phone calls or letters. It was the late 60's and it was possible to avoid indefinitely a person's efforts to communicate. He spent his days riding his motorcycle, flying around curves and down hills just outside of the city, turning over in his mind everything he thought he knew about this girl he loved. He refused to believe she could be this cruel.

The boy lay awake each night in his bedroom, trying to relive and analyze every moment of that visit to her home. He had not told her that he was coming, nor had he told her about the ring he had picked out and put a deposit on. In his mind, a surprise proposal in her childhood home would create a heartwarming chapter in their history, a touchstone memory that they could call up throughout their lives together. Yes, they were very young, but he felt his reasoning was sound. They were madly in love. And the December lottery had not been in his favor. His number was 83, and even though he had a student deferment for the time being, it could be just a matter of months before he would be drafted.

They had talked far into the nights they shared together at Fredonia about how the world was falling apart around them. All they had to do was turn on the television or read a newspaper to have that verified. Before they had met, as young teens, they had each watched the footage of their beloved president being assassinated over and over again on what seemed like endless hours of film. Walter Cronkite reported on the hunt for the three Freedom Riders who had disappeared in Mississippi, and the subsequent burning of the cities across the country; they had watched that too. And now, during their college years, supposedly the best years of their lives, there was Vietnam. Each night dozens of kids gathered around the television in the Gregory Hall student union to watch burning villages and American boys being shipped home in body bags.

The boy was certain that in the midst of all this chaos, their commitment to one another would be a grounding force. They could stand up to life's brutalities and make the world a better place. So, he filled his gas tank and drove south and then east on Route 17 to her home, buoyant with optimism and love.

His arrival had taken her by surprise; she had looked shocked when she opened the door to him, alone in the house. He could see that she was nervous about her parents' response to his just showing up without warning. But then they had been alone for a few hours, and their lovemaking had seemed to quell any doubts she had about introducing him to them this way. And when he had proposed to her while they were still in her bed, she had said yes.

So, why had she not stood with him on her porch that morning after? Why was she not in touch with him now? It had to be her father. Although she had never revealed it, as he thought about it now, he was sure he must be a domineering son-of-a-bitch. Well, the boy had wanted her parents' blessing; he knew she was especially close to her old man. The absence of a father in his own life, the boy reasoned, made it even more important that they had Mr. Fray's approval. But, of course, as far as New York State was concerned, they were of age and could marry without his consent. He thought about that on his ride back to Utica, and that fact was reassuring. But the girl's silence during the rest of the week was torturous.

An eternity seemed to pass before the day came that he could get back to school and their life together. He was anxious throughout his mother's chatter as she drove him to catch the bus at the downtown station. He was distracted when he said goodbye to her. Usually, he would sleep for most of the six-hour ride across the state. But he could not shut his mind off, although he was completely exhausted from his lack of sleep throughout the week. He tried to read, but he could not concentrate.

When the bus pulled onto the tree-lined campus, he felt a comforting rush of familiarity wash over him. As he looked out of the Greyhound window, he was aware of how much the college had changed, was continuing to change, since he had first come as a freshman. The age of each building could be easily identified as either "old campus" or "new campus;" the original ten red brick buildings stood in stark contrast to the new IM Pei designed concrete architecture, whose construction was underway. New roads were being dug, too, so the walk from one class to the next could be a muddy endeavor.

The bus stopped and pulled up to the curb nearest to the dormitories. The boy looked out the window at his dorm building and felt better than he had all week. This place was their *real* home, his and his girl's. It was a fortress, barring them from the intrusions of the outside world, and that included the disapproval of parents. They were free to be themselves here, to move forward in their lives as they saw fit.

He threw his bag on the bed in his dorm room and ran across the green to her residence hall. In the lobby, he used the house phone and called her room. Her roommate, Susan, answered. His girl did not have much in common with her, they did not hang out with the same people, and for the most part, they just tolerated one another. But somehow, as she spoke to him, he believed every word she said. "Hey. Look, I'm supposed to tell you she's not here yet, but she is. She's seriously trying to avoid you, man. She's a coward. But she told me it's over. She's done with you."

The words hit him like a punch in the gut. His legs actually felt wobbly; he sat down on the oversized leather sofa in the common area of her dorm. He could not for the life of him figure out what had happened, but now that they were back on campus, he could no longer blame her callousness on her family's disapproval of him.

The boy walked back to his room and flopped down on the bed and fell asleep. He awoke, blurry-headed. When he could think again, he decided that the last thing he wanted to do was appear desperate to the girl. He would give her some space. She would miss him and what they had together, he was so sure of that. One day soon she would call him or come to his dorm, or he would find her waiting outside of a classroom for him. In the meantime, although it was not his style, he would be patient.

For the rest of the semester, he caught only glimpses of her, in the Union, where she had whispered that she loved him only weeks before, walking across campus, in the bars downtown, always in the company of a blockade of friends who were strangers to him, male and female. He felt invisible. Night after night, he got so drunk and high, he spent most of that late spring term stupefied. Blissful sleep came to him eventually when he got that blitzed. He slept through classes and then through finals.

By the time he went home for the summer to his mom's lonely house, he had a perpetual case of hives. He had lost ten pounds. His long hair was falling out in chunks. And he had flunked out.

Unbeknownst to him, his mother, desperate on behalf of her only child, had written a letter to the girl's parents, the way they would have done it in the old country. She told them he was a good boy, a smart young man, and a hard worker. He would make a wonderful husband. Why would they not let him see their daughter? There never was a reply.

And then the letter from Selective Service came for him. There was a scheduled physical, and now that he was no longer enrolled in school, the likelihood was great that he would be drafted. What the hell, he thought. He would enlist. There was nothing stopping him, nothing, really, to live for.

So he had volunteered for this next chapter in his life, even though it was a radical departure from what he had expected his path to be. For the past year, he had been involved in the beginnings of the Peace Movement on campus, and now he was signing up for combat.

First, there was a tour of duty in the Mekong Delta, and then three more years of service. To hell and back home to Utica in four years; that was how he summed up his time in the army to anyone who asked.

Decades passed. Like most people, life brought him some joy, but more sorrow. Because of his failures as a young man, he became a person who questioned his worthiness. His outlook was often clouded by this doubt. During especially difficult years, he returned to the bad habits he had picked up during his time in Vietnam; he drugged himself, he drank too much. Other years, mainly for the sake of his wife and daughters, he got himself together and found his sobriety again. He went to meetings and kept appointments with his various counselors at the VA.

Throughout all of these times, good and bad, he often felt like he was just going through the motions of living. He was breathing someone else's air, following a stranger's path. He was a pretender, a very bad actor. Where was the man he had started out to be? Had he let it get away from him then, his real life?

By the time he turned 50, these questions stayed mainly in the background of his day-to-day life, an annoying, buzzing static. He stayed sober, mostly, and that helped him to focus on the present, no matter how mundane and vacuous it seemed. But occasionally, he had sleepless nights, and then, when sleep came to him, some of the old nightmares from long ago returned too.

Each time he searched and probed for the key to this recurring anxiety, he visualized his twenty-year-old self back on the girl's porch in the Catskills. If only he could return to that day and solve the puzzle, perhaps he could transform the events of his life from that time forward. What had changed her mind and heart? He knew that if he could find the answer to that, he could fix every broken thing about him.

Then he turned 60, and because he had taken up running and weight lifting in the last couple of years, he felt like he was in the best shape of his life. In spite of this, at his annual physical, his doctor was not happy with the appearance of an odd-shaped mole on his left cheek. He sent Phil to a dermatologist. The results of the biopsy were not what he had hoped for. A specialist's second opinion was followed by a surgery and then a blurry diagnosis. He might be able to beat this, but a recurrence would not be a good sign.

He pictured the foreign thing that had been inside him as her old man. When he was feeling good, he knew he would prevail. But when he was having a shitty day, the son-of-a-bitch was throwing him off that porch all over again.

Chapter Two — The House

Leigh Ann tossed her keys into the wooden bowl on the kitchen counter and assured her three cats that they would be fed. She flicked the lighter and fired up the residual pot in the bowl of her newest glass pipe. She inhaled deeply and glanced around the room. She loved this old house of hers, perhaps more than any other she had lived in. It held everything she needed to remind her of the best moments of her past, but in the two years since acquiring it, she had shared its warm space with no one. She made good on the promise to her cats, set the pipe down after taking another hit, and walked through the dining room into the narrow hallway leading to her study.

She paused to admire for the thousandth time the photo gallery she had lovingly arranged in this space when she had first bought the place. Framed pictures of cups of cappuccino she had drunk all over Europe, their foamy tops artfully shaped into hearts, flowers, maps of Italy. A collage of the women in her life, her mother in her high school cap and gown; her grandmother, who had taken her to Italy for the first time when she had turned seventeen – they stood with their arms around each other in St. Mark's Square. Two of her childhood friends in one and an eight by ten of her three college roommates, all with whom she still kept in close contact. Hanging on the opposite wall was a mini-gallery dedicated to her children. She missed her son and daughter, now both musicians with decent paying day jobs and both living on the west coast.

Lilly and David had been told by their parents that they could do and be anything. As Leigh Ann looked from their baby pictures to the posters from each of their bands, she knew they had grown up believing that.

She walked into her study, her favorite space in the house. Sitting down at her desk she turned on her laptop and opened the link to the latest edition of *The Ellicottville Courier.* The newspaper that she wrote for was first and foremost a publication aimed at the Canadian tourists and seasonal residents who skied the charming village's mountains in the winter and golfed its beautiful courses in the summer. The paper's mission was to inform those who had much discretionary cash how and where they could spend it. Most of the articles were nothing more than print infomercials featuring reviews of the local bars and restaurants. Except for Leigh Ann's column. She had been invited to join the staff a few years back as their resident scholar, and because she had wanted the opportunity to write something outside of the academic realm, she had accepted.

Occasionally, she would write a book or film review, or she might use her space to launch into some aspect of her passion for Arthurian literature in a "user-friendly" style, as her editor had gently suggested. But more typically, her column elaborated upon the same theme, a conviction that Leigh Ann had long held. She believed whole-heartedly in the magic that fate and coincidence could bring, the cosmic nature of chance convergences. Almost every month, she wrote an eloquent observation of the intriguing intertwinings that fate could produce, more often than not, based upon her own first-hand observations. Her writing had garnered a small, but loyal following. When she retired from teaching, she planned on collating thirty of her best essays and submitting the collection for publication, as she had often been encouraged by her enthusiastic readers to do.

Her latest effort, however, had been the most intimate and self-revealing piece she had ever written; she had dropped all of her usual objectivity and directly invited her readers into her life. She had petitioned their advice, and now she was rereading the column and searching for their remarks with a mixture of excitement and dread.

CONVERGENCES

Don't Know Much About History
by Leigh Ann Fray

For those of you who may have read my column more than once, based on this month's title, you may be steeling yourself for yet another of my obsessive forays into all -things-Tudor. Hopefully, you will not be disappointed as you read, not about Henry's loves, conquests, and ill-fated marriages, but of my own.

I am, as of last month, officially divorced. It has taken six years. A glacial speed, even in New York State, I know. But suffice it to say, until the last two, I could not reconcile the two ideas, me and divorce. Although I am a product of the sixties, I have always viewed the marriage vow as the most serious of commitments, impermeable and eternal, as surprisingly straight-laced as that may seem to those of you who share my more typical liberal beliefs.

But "_____ (insert the level of profanity you are comfortable with here) happens," my students always say, as they tell or write their own sad stories. We have all faced adversity and tragedy, and I have certainly struggled with my own. The fortress that was my marriage is no more. At last I can say, it's for the best. And I have come a long way to that realization, as my friends and family can tell you.

But the part of this schism that will never stop causing me pain is the notion that my partner of 25 years is no longer a co-author and historian of the long life that we shared. Without him, I am on my own in terms of recalling and reliving the small and monumental that make a life. *What was that guy's name in Dr. Wilson's Myths and Legends course who used to bring his parrot to class? Was my grandmother at our wedding, or was she gone by then? Remember that horrible little kitchen we had in Kingston? Who was that amazing guitarist we saw at Levon Helm's place when we lived in Woodstock? When we took the kids to New York that summer, how did we dare bring a 12 and 14 year old into CBGB's? What kind of woman was I in my thirties? Did you think I was beautiful, ever?*

Those of you kids out there who are 50 and under probably have clear recollections of most of the events of your lives. But those of us who were teens during the British Invasion (musical, not military, my young readers) know what it's like to lose sections or whole chapters of our story. Your life's partner might have been an active accomplice, or at the very least, a witness to these times, the trivial and the significant.

That's what I miss, now that I am at last divorced. It's admittedly self-centered, but I am missing, not him, but parts of myself and my story that cannot be recovered.

That is why I am considering the idea of reconnecting with a man from my LONG AGO, BEFORE-MARRIAGE- AND- KIDS past.

I received an email a couple of weeks ago from a man who was looking for "a long lost friend" who had attended Fredonia State in 1968, and asking, if I was that same Leigh Ann Fray, would I be interested in getting together? In our few exchanges, I've discovered that he certainly does remember more than I about the time we shared so long ago, when I was a "pretty young girl," and he was a hippie with shoulder-length hair and cool John Lennon glasses. Most intriguing to me is the fact that he has wanted for a "very long time" to have a conversation about "what happened those many years ago."

Again, my memory has failed me. I recall only how adorable I thought Phil was, so much so that I accepted, though warily, his invitation to hitchhike to Syracuse to see Jimmy Hendrix at the Aud. I have vague memories of being on the Thruway and catching a ride with a family in a station wagon. I remember bits and pieces of the concert that has trumped all of my friends' musical experiences from that era (except for Kathy, who had seen the Beatles in Toronto). And I remember his showing up unannounced at my home during the spring break that followed the concert. My parents were not impressed. In fact, when I told my youngest brother about these recent email exchanges, he shared his clear memory of seeing our father toss this boy off of our front porch. Shortly after that "visit," I reconnected, for a short time anyway, with my high school boyfriend, who was conventional and safe. When I went back to college after that break, Phil seemed to have disappeared.

And now, out of the cyberspace blue, he has materialized forty years later. And so, I have spent too much time alone mulling over this question: If I invite him to visit, will he help me to recall 1968 and the 18 -year- old me?

Dear readers, those of you who respond regularly, and others who may be first time commentators, I have a favor to ask of you. Weigh in on my dilemma, if you are moved to do so. Shall I invite him to come so we can have this "conversation?" Would his view of our youth help me to see more clearly the Leigh Ann I was then? Or do you think, as Thomas Wolfe said, you can't go home again?
Until next month…

Write a comment

Read 5 comments

JP Jude - Cassadaga

Leigh Ann, sorry about your divorce, it's a tough thing, but you have your whole life ahead of you. Stop looking back.

Ski Bum - Toronto

Last year I went to my 50th year class reunion. Next weekend I am marrying my high school sweetheart; you go, girl!

Cool Hunter - Hinsdale

Leigh Ann. I have taken several of your courses at ACC. You are a strong, intelligent, beautiful woman. No man deserves you.

Wise Guy- Ellicottville

He sounds like he could be a creep. Caveat Emptor!

Peaceloveandunderstanding- Portville

Do you really want to relive 1968? Hendrix was about the only bright light; MLK and then RFK, Vietnam. I was there too, and I really prefer the 21st century.

Well, she thought, as she closed out the site, it could have been a lot worse. These days, it seemed that every crackpot in the country felt free to express in a blog or a comment any crap that came into their heads, and her own writing, although infrequently, had been on the receiving end of some of it. Leigh Ann could picture these jerks, hiding behind their screen names, using their anonymous voices. More often than not, they made facile judgments and broad pronouncements. But sometimes she detected a pathology in their words, or at the very least an emotional instability. As a matter of fact, since she had submitted this latest column, she had reread Phil Perrero's most recent email several times, and with each reading, her unease had grown. She wasn't sure that her old college flame had not joined the ranks of these nut cases.

She scrolled through her Inbox and found Phil's last message. She donned her composition teacher's hat and began to read. Right away, she was put off by a misspelling and a few grammatical errors, and the elitist in her bristled at some of his elementary syntax. She had tried to overlook these flaws when she had first read his messages; Leigh Ann had been a Match.com drop-out after a month of hearing from men who could not spell, never mind write a coherent sentence. It was a personal bias, and perhaps it was not fair to discount the man behind the lousy sentence structure.

So she started to read again, for content this time. Most of the message was quite flattering, maybe that's why she had initially overlooked other parts of it that now caused a quiet alarm to go off inside her. He had made clear that he was married, a fact that she had left out in her *Convergences* column. So what did he really want from her? Yeah, definitely, she thought to herself as she continued to read. There were portions of it that might have been written by someone who was not quite stable. He wanted to have a "hard conversation," he needed some answers from her. Damn! Why had she ever responded to his first few attempts to reconnect? If Peter had been here, he would have told her that she was a sitting duck for this kind of creep to slither his way back into her life... thank God, Peter was not here!

Since their divorce, her life had changed drastically. She had sold the four bedroom American Four Square home where the kids had grown up in Ellicottville, and bought this cozy Batten and Board original within walking distance of her campus in Allegany. The house had served as a modest rectory when it had been built in the nineteenth century; the concrete carriage block still stood by her front curb, 1872 etched into it. The perennial garden in the back included magnificent rhododendron that had to be at least one hundred years old.

Before she had moved in, she had enlisted a couple of students who needed the money to help her paint walls and tear up carpets. She hired a local company to strip and varnish the wide-planked floors that had lay beneath the smelly rugs. The husband of a colleague who was an architect helped her to design and remodel the kitchen so that it functioned beyond perfunctory tasks. She loved to cook, and she made herself beautiful meals when the teaching week was over, and often she invited small groups of friends to join her. Leigh Ann had appreciated the distraction the process of renovating had brought her. The undertaking had eased her over the threshold from married to single.

Although she didn't think she would ever get rid of the nagging feeling that the dissolution of her marriage was a personal failing, she had learned surprisingly quickly to enjoy, and then to love, her solitary life. No compromises had to be made, no having to adjust her behavior or opinions so that day-to-day living was tolerable. Leigh Ann knew there were many times in her life when she had not stood on her own two feet and dealt head on with people, mainly because she detested conflict. Predictably, her therapist who she saw during her separation from Peter, viewed this behavior as a throwback to her relationship with her alcoholic mother. Yes, throughout childhood and beyond Leigh Ann had second-guessed herself, caved and given in, just to keep Katy Fray off of her back. And this strategy had seemed to be useful in her relationships with other people, women and men, but especially with Peter.

Leigh Ann realized her passivity could be seen as a dichotomy. How could an intelligent, professional woman be so weak, and from time to time, so downright disingenuous? When she was in graduate school in Albany, she had been a part of the Feminist movement (for God's sake, how many other women had bought and still owned that first copy of Ms. Magazine with the incredible Gloria Steinem on the cover?) and most people who knew her - friends, colleagues, and students alike, thought of her as a strong woman. But Peter had pointed out many times throughout their marriage that although she wore the mask of the feminist, she was a fraud. She was a phony people pleaser and a world-class procrastinator, according to her husband. She had accepted his judgment, and gone on with her life, dodging conflict whenever she could. But now, Peter and his pronouncements were missing from her life, and she was starting anew.

Independence was scary for Leigh Ann in many ways, but it provided her with the space to start looking back at the decisions that had been made for her in the past. Her parents, boyfriends, husband, bosses, sometimes even students had filled in the void left by her passivity with their own choices. Now at 58, living on her own, she felt like she was actually growing a backbone; it was time she discovered what she truly needed and wanted out of what was left of her life.

The arrival of Phil's emails had coincided with a growing restlessness, an urge to share at least some of her newly emerging self with a man. So that timing had gone in his favor, that and Leigh Ann's belief in the power of fate's convergences. She had been flattered because he had still thought about her all these years later, and there had been their shared history at Fredonia, a place and time she valued. All of this had led her to a rather hasty decision to answer his first querying correspondence. She had been thinking it was time to connect with a man, a potential partner, and here was one asking for a reunion. But as she reread this last email, she was sure that Phil Perrero would not be that man.

She would answer his email, and turn down his request for an invitation to visit her, but she would not write it today. She had the whole weekend ahead of her to compose it, she assured herself. And she would be open and honest with him when she did.

Spooky, the oldest and most demanding of her feline menagerie wailed to be let outside. Somehow, she had inherited her kids' cats, along with all the boxes of their stuff she had moved from Ellicottville and now stored in the attic.

Just as she opened the front door to let the insistent cat out, the old-fashioned buzzer, the kind that had to be twisted into use, assaulted her ears and she stifled a scream. Standing on her porch in her emergency-orange Kwik Fill uniform and clutching a back pack was the most troubled student Leigh Ann had had in her forty years of teaching.

"Can I *please* stay here tonight?"

Chapter Three — Braggadocios

The Voice had been persistent. It urged, in its steady hum and reasonable tone, that Charlotte must help Leigh Ann. Throughout three sleepless nights and two shifts at The Kwik Fill, the girl had tried to shut it out. But the Voice had been relentless and, finally, convincing. Charlotte had crammed her backpack with everything she would need. Three changes of clothes, the $300 she had saved, printed copies of Leigh Ann's *Convergences* columns from the past three years, and her father's old .38 along with a box containing several rounds of ammunition.

Now she leveraged her one hundred and twenty pound advantage and pushed past the shocked teacher, crossing the threshold of this woman who needed her protection. "Good work," the Voice said.

"No! Charlotte, we've had this conversation before. I can't let you stay here!" Leigh Ann had rocked back on her heels when the girl pushed past her. It was difficult to sound resolute from this position. She steadied herself by holding onto the doorframe. In her most assertive voice she said, "You can't be here!"

"You're in," the Voice said to the girl. "Now do what you came to do."

Charlotte had first enrolled in Leigh Ann's Developmental Reading and Writing course as an 18 year old two years earlier. She had, during those subsequent two years, taken every class that the professor taught, at least once, sometimes three times. She was a total devotee, not of learning, but of Leigh Ann. From that first day in her first class, Charlotte listened and watched intently as the animated teacher shared anecdotes about her own college years, the concerts she had attended, her travels, the places where she had lived and taught before coming to this rather forlorn upstate community twenty years ago with her husband and children. Charlotte felt as though it was just the two of them in the room as Leigh Ann proudly revealed much about her children (way too much if you asked Lilly and David) about their high school and college escapades, their exploits on the west coast, their tattoos, their careers as musicians. But she also made it clear that, in her class, this sharing would be a two-way exchange. She was the type of teacher who would listen respectfully to their opinions and insights on writing and literature, and if they were moved to share personal and emotional reactions, her kindness assured them that her classroom was a safe place for these exchanges as well. Leigh Ann's warmth opened up a portal to Charlotte's broken core. The girl felt something stirring inside her, primal and extraordinary.

At the bottom of her course syllabus the professor listed her office hours and number, as was standard practice for all faculty, but Leigh Ann always included her cell number, as well, with the caveat that the students use it only for "writing emergencies." Charlotte entered both numbers into her cell phone contact list before that first class had ended.

Charlotte wore thick glasses and a perpetual frown. She was unkempt and unhealthily overweight. In this first decade of the 21st century, she was a singular character in every way, and she was accustomed to being avoided by others. She walked across campus alone, she sat in the student union alone. When she spoke in class, which was often, much to the chagrin of her classmates, her voice was loud and grating. She could be rude, and her commentary during most classroom discussion was clearly braggadocio and sometimes downright bizarre. If another student mentioned that she had been a reporter on her high school newspaper, Charlotte claimed to have been the editor of hers. If someone had seen a play in Buffalo, she had tickets to see a musical on Broadway. If a classmate had gone winter camping, she claimed to have been lost in the Allegany Forest and to have found her way out of the wilderness without a GPS. All of this was expressed in a tone of voice that suggested that all of these people who were not Charlotte were assholes.

Leigh Ann, like the students, found Charlotte to be an unappealing character, but the girl's presence in her classroom roiled up an ambivalence in the teacher. Her maternal instinct would flare when an audible snicker followed one of the girl's outrageous lies; but in the next minute, Leigh Ann felt an unavoidable wave of disgust sweep over her when she looked at this pathetic person.

Although Charlotte was unaware of these negative feelings on her beloved teacher's part, she was quite familiar with the revulsion she caused in most people, even her parents. She had woken up one morning in February when she was nine years old to find that her mother had left the five of them with their "loser" (the word she had screamed at him two nights previous) of a father. He had worked for the railroad many years before her mother left, but then he had hurt his back. Since then, he had been receiving monthly disability checks. As far back as Charlotte could remember, his only work regimen had been the hunting and fishing he did to supplement the food stamp staples. His drinking was done in binges; on a daily basis, however, the children experienced his seething sobriety.

They lived on the family homestead in a dilapidated 20th century farmhouse that her grandfather had built. By the time Charlotte was born, the barns and outbuildings were more like piles of tinder, rather than working structures, as they had originally been intended. The acreage that surrounded the house was wooded with pine, spruce, maple and oak. A stream ran through the property, providing them with some trout and catfish. In the summers, there was a poorly tended vegetable garden.

Although her family struggled no more than their neighbors, because they were motherless, they had an additional disadvantage. The cruelest of children sensed the vulnerability of the Whites, sniffed it out like vultures to raw flesh. Charlotte and her siblings were badgered and harassed throughout their school years, inside and outside of that yellow chamber of horrors, the school bus. And when they arrived at the old brick building that served as the elementary, middle, and high schools, life became pure hell for Charlotte. She had difficulty reading, and math may as well have been taught in Latin. She was tested and retested throughout her early school years, but these tools determined that she had no special needs.

Because she was the oldest in her family, her childhood ended when her mother left. The house became her responsibility, as did the cooking for her father and little brothers and sisters. Cleaning was optional, since the "standard" was set by a man who was totally indifferent to filth and often blinded by drink. Any resemblance to cleanliness was maintained by children who were pretty much left to their own resort. By the time she was in middle school, the place was in such a shambles most of the time, Charlotte was too ashamed to bring anyone else inside. Whenever a potential playmate asked if she could come to her house, Charlotte's ready-made lie was that they were "remodeling," a concept she had learned from her mother's habitual watching of DIY television.

Had her father been abusive? Years later, when Leigh Ann asked her this question during their conference about her first composition assignment, Charlotte struggled to do something that did not come easily to her. She tried to tell the truth. No, he had never touched her in any inappropriate way, although she had squeamishly witnessed some mouth kisses he had planted on her little sister once after a night out at the bar. But he had left them, often, to fend for themselves. There was a time when Charlotte was in middle school that he drove off and didn't return for three days. The children had eaten all of the cold cuts and drunk the milk, then eaten the bread, then all of the dry cereal.

On the third morning of his absence, Charlotte awoke to a panicky desperation, a state of consciousness that could overtake her with no provocation from that point on throughout her life. Terror-stricken beyond tears, Charlotte and her brother Bud headed to the stream behind the house. The one thing her father had felt obligated to teach them was how to hunt and fish. The two children managed to catch three decent-sized trout. She skinned and gutted them as her father had shown her. Thank God there was propane left in the stove.

As the five of them sat at the kitchen table wolfing down the first protein they had had during his hiatus, they heard his pick-up in the driveway. Charlotte looked out the window as her father walked hand-in-hand toward the house with an orange-haired stranger.

Several weird women came and went throughout Charlotte's childhood. Some of them were nice to her, others simply acted as though she and her siblings didn't exist. Most of them left after a day or two of partying with her father. This one stayed for a couple of miserable months. Her name was Bridget, and she tried to assert her authority, such as it was, over this girl who had been in charge of not only her own life, but that of her siblings for several years. Her father watched passively as Bridget slapped Charlotte for back talking or giving her dirty looks. At night, Charlotte stayed out of her way, although Bridget, like her father, was meaner when she was sober.

As Charlotte entered adolescence, she felt her father's indifference toward her grow. She had begged him to go to open houses and parent conferences during elementary and middle school, but he had always refused. When the official forms and teachers' notes expressing concern were sent home during her high school years, they, too, were ignored. One morning, after many failed attempts to reach Charlotte's father by phone, the school nurse drove out to their house, and Bill White came to the door. She told him that Charlotte had failed a routine eye exam that the school physician had given to every high school freshman. Her vision had worsened drastically since her last pair of glasses was purchased by the state. The nurse urged him to take Charlotte to the optometrist. And so, because her father didn't want any one nosing into his business, or showing up at his house without an invitation, he took her to the eye doctor. Charlotte put on the thick coke bottle glasses that set her apart her from her contact-lens-wearing peers.

Her height and weight gain during this time necessitated her foraging through her mother's clothes thrown angrily in boxes by her father years before. The jeans barely fit, but she could use an elastic extender at the waist. The shirts and dresses were mainly floral prints, which made her look, not "retro", but crazy. Her body and "style" were easy targets for high school critics, who laughed behind her back. But by this time, she was not bullied in the physical sense. Most of her peers were wary of her stature and her quick anger. She stared down anyone who looked at her too long, and when they did not look away, she felt a rage that was palpable and violent. They mainly stayed a safe distance away from her and amused themselves with "Mad Charlotte " imitations, with which by her senior year, they had grown bored.

It was at about this time in her life that Charlotte started hearing the Voice beyond the walls of her bedroom, during the daylight hours, as well. She had read about and seen movies where crazy people heard voices in their heads. But her Voice was not a muse for the insane. It was very much in control. First, she would hear a low buzzing sound and then the Voice would speak. It was not a human voice, rather it had a robotic quality. It was quiet and confident, and this assertiveness was what soothed Charlotte when she was confronted with the nastiness that was her life. The Voice told her not to worry about her father's laziness and apathy, or the sounds coming out of his bedroom when one of his whores was there. The Voice assured her that her classmates were garbage and it would be alright to scream at, kick, hit, punch any one of them, if they came too close. At night, the Voice would collaborate with her when she was trying to plan an escape route from her misery.

When she turned 17, she wanted to get her license so that she could get a job. The Whites lived six miles away from town, so the license was a necessity. "We only have the pick up. What am I supposed to do while you're earning $6 an hour? And what happens when you wreck it? I can't afford a new vehicle," her father said. She did not argue with him. This was the most he had spoken to her in a very long time, and she knew he would have not expended the effort if he had not meant it. The Voice agreed with her: Charlotte had no license, no job, no hope.

Throughout the spring of her wretched senior year, she often fantasized about the thing her father kept in his bedroom closet. The object that could take away her pain. Each night before she fell asleep, the Voice would lead her through the steps she would have to take to reach her goal. First, she would sneak into his room and get the loaded gun off the shelf. She would leave a note on the seat of her father's pick-up telling him where he would find her, so that none of the little kids would discover her body first. She would walk in the dark to the furthest outbuilding on their property. She had hunted with a shotgun many times and she and her brother had used the handgun to target practice with their father from the time she was ten. It was the only solution, the Voice told her, and it would *not* be the hardest thing she had had to do in her seventeen years.

She and the Voice chose a date in June, just before graduation. The three little kids would be getting out of school soon after and Bud could take over some of her household duties. The Voice assured her nightly that she had nothing to live for and would not be missed.

Sitting in her social studies class the day before final exams began, Charlotte was startled by the school secretary's voice coming over the PA. "Will the following students please report to the guidance office when the bell rings." The names of three other seniors were read and then "Charlotte White." She had no idea why she was a part of this group, or that she was about to be granted a reprieve from the punishment that was her life.

She sat across the desk from Mr. Burgess. The guidance counselor was a huge man, who for some reason, was constantly wiping his mouth with a handkerchief. The kids called him Spitty because of this habit. He put it back in his pocket now and smiled at

47

her. "Don't look so glum, Charlotte. It's good news."
He explained that because of her family's income level,
she was qualified to attend Allegany Community
College tuition-free, as long as she remained a county
citizen. She would also have to maintain a 2.5 grade
point average each semester, which he believed she
could do if she studied and worked very hard.

She walked out of the guidance office, beaming,
right into the path of one of her few classmates who
actually spoke to her. "What's up, White?" he asked,
surprised by the look of delight on this angry girl's face.

"I just found out I have a full scholarship to
Allegany!" The lie bounced off the walls of the empty
corridor.

He smiled as he goaded her. "Wow! I thought
you hated school and that you were going to live in New
York City once you got out of this hellhole,"

She *had* hated high school, but the alternative
was to have to cook, clean, and take care of her siblings
full time. She would have to put up with her father's
apathy and his crazy, drunken bitches. She would be
stuck, maybe forever, in that miserable place, in her
unhappy life. And the Voice had agreed that that would
be her fate.

But that day, Charlotte had been given an acquittal from her wretched future, and now she would have a new life, one worth living. She would be a college student. She had had no desire before this day to go beyond high school. And so she could not fathom what life after college would be, but this amazing turn of events was enough. Her brother Bud had his license now, and her father had bought a new pickup, so Bud had been given the old one. All that spring, her brother had driven them into town each day to go to the high school. In the fall, they could work something out so that she could be dropped off and stay in town until he could pick her up. Maybe she would even get a job.

After that day, probably the most exciting day of Charlotte's life, the Voice was silent for the rest of the summer. She remained alert each night for the buzzing in her ears that always preceded It, but It did not come. She tried with all her power to summon It, but It was quiet.

That August, Charlotte registered for classes at ACC, and within the week, she sat in a front desk staring up at the woman upon whose life she would bring devastation.

Chapter Four — Devastation

Phil was nauseous. He staggered through the endless mud into the darkness. The M-16 with the night scope he had carried for the last two hours felt like a fucking crucifix. His fire team was following the stench emanating from the canal to the hamlet of Ap Bac. The tiny village had become a funeral pyre their bomber comrades had lit earlier in the day. The stink of decay and smoke combined and exacerbated his queasiness. He had dreaded this night. The action he was going to have to take tonight would change his life forever, perhaps destroy him. But he had had enough.

That morning, in this place and all over the province, leaflets had swirled down out of the bowels of three choppers as the loudspeaker blared in the language of the people. **"Citizens of Dinh Tuong. You are residing in a Free Fire Zone. The South Vietnam People's Republic orders you to pack your belongings and go to the nearest Citizens' Relocation Camp. You must vacate in the next three hours."**

The amplified strangeness of the vernacular interrupted Phil's concentration. Lying on his bunk in the Fire Support Base, he was listening to the Youngbloods on AFVN. He had seen them last year at Fredonia when they had toured the US. That Phil, pleasantly stoned and sitting next to the pretty Leigh Ann, could have never imagined that *Darkness, Darkness* would become the anthem of his twentieth year and all of the years that followed.

Darkness, Darkness, be my pillow

Take my head and let me sleep

In the coolness of your shadow, In the silence of your deep

Darkness, darkness, hide my yearning

For the things I cannot see

Keep my mind from constant turning, To the things I cannot be

Darkness, darkness, be my blanket, cover me with the endless night

Take away the pain of knowing, fill the emptiness of fright

Emptiness of fright

Brian Kopliner, his buddy from Austin, turned away from the ragged issue of Playboy his brother had sent him months before. "Hey, Hippie. Sounds like we're going snipe hunting again tonight." Phil's stomach did a sickening flip-flop.

Now, as they walked alongside the rice paddies, the smoke hung in the humid air. The usual nighttime music of this country, an exotic cacophony of insects and other creatures that kept Phil awake most nights when he wasn't on duty, was absent. He watched, his nerves on fire, as their point man, Leonard Dietrich, silently gestured for the six of them to follow him through a fruit orchard, where an outlying hut still stood. Phil felt the vomit rise up into his throat as he trailed this faction of his unit.

Sergeant Dietrich was a firm believer in the body count maxim: the more they produced, the sooner they would be out of the field and this hellhole of a country, and he repeatedly conveyed this principle to his men. "When the corpse census is taken, no one will ask if they're VC troops or farmers," he said, each time they went out on one of these night sweeps. "A dead Gook is a dead Gook. The eradication of the civilians who are enemy sympathizers is a key component to the success of this operation. What we do matters! This war cannot be won without us! Don't ever forget that," he would bark.

Dietrich, a stocky, blond Chicagoan, served and led by the MGR maxim taught in basic training to all who were being deployed. At Fort Riley, Phil too, had been instructed in The Mere Gook Rule. The fundamental tenet was explained by a tactical specialist who had just returned from Kien Ho. "You have to move beyond the notion that these are people. The inhabitants of this country are sub-human. They are filthy because they have no standards of hygiene. They are ignorant. But they are ruthless, like wild animals would be if you got too close. They smile at you, and then they stab you. They are not like you or me in any way. You will never think or refer to them to as Vietnamese, but as Slopes, Gooks, and Chinks," the corporal had said, as he drilled the army's newest inductees.

Phil could feel the hairs on the back of his neck bristle throughout these lectures. His first generation American sensibilities were rattled. "Put yourself in the other guy's shoes," his mother had often told him in her thick Italian accent throughout his boyhood. She had grown up in a country where, all too often, the common people were the sacrificial lambs of prejudice and brutality. She had taught Phil that compassion should be extended to playground bullies, as well as to their victims. Margaret Perrero explained that Phil's father, who had been a POW in Germany at the end of the Second World War, was especially in need of his unmitigated empathy. His son had no memory of the man. He had simply walked away from them when Phil was a baby. "Put yourself in his shoes," his mother told her little son, anytime he asked why his dad was not there with them. Margaret was horrified when her only child had enlisted and deployed. She knew too well how war could destroy a man.

Phil would never tell his mother about the black pajama clad farmers from villages close to the base that he and his comrades had encountered and dealt with in their duties as infantrymen. The United States Army believed that most of these civilians were Communist sympathizers, and so they ordered everyone in these hamlets to the closest relocation centers in the province; but there were always a few people who did not want to leave their farms and rice paddies, the fishing in the canals, their ancestral burial plots. They knew that their small piece of this delta land would more than likely be claimed by others once they abandoned it. Only the strongest and most stubborn among them hid during these evacuations.

And Phil's battalion would always find stragglers; sometimes several, more often dozens. He would not tell his mother the rules of the macabre ritual in which he participated during those three months; over and over again, in the name of the great country to which she had immigrated as a teenager, Phil played his part. First, each member of the unit would put his weapon on full automatic, as he had been ordered to do, so as to take out the greatest number of those who dared to flee. Next, each infantryman would pick out an individual to stare down. As soon as one man, woman, or child risked running, that movement would inevitably trigger a chain reaction of escape. It was most often the case that the old men and women stood their ground longest, so if the soldiers felt like speeding up this maneuver, they would select a young boy to fix their eyes upon. Soon after the most skittish boy had been chosen and attempted to flee, the explosions of M-16's filled the air. From his first night sweep to his last, Phil always lingered on the edge of this horrifying game of chicken, shaking. He would fire his weapon at invisible civilians on the outskirts of the event, or into the air, if he felt it would go unnoticed by the rest of the team.

And in the aftermath, he watched as husbands, wives, kids, grandparents, toddlers, infants lay mortally wounded, burned and mutilated, dead and dying. It always seemed to him that they fell together in circles, head or feet facing in, like the weirdest of family reunions. Over and over again, the families fell. Over and over again, as he watched them die, Phil felt like an intruder upon an intimate gathering.

Phil could not tell his mother about the "celebration" in My Tho that he had been a part of just weeks before he was sent out of country to his base in Hawaii. Kopliner had scored some powerful Nam Black the day before, and after smoking it most of the morning, he, Phil, Dietrich, along with the rest of their team, John Graziano, from Cleveland, and Sid Pouthier, from Minneapolis, decided to drive into the province capital for some fun and relaxation. Phil stayed high, very high, as much as and for as long as was possible during his time in country, earning his Hippie moniker. The college freaks that he had gotten blasted with could not have dreamed of the varieties or the potency of weed that was readily available here. And on this day, in particular, Phil was happy to be blissfully blitzed.

Dietrich was the only one of them with a military driver's license, so he steered the Jeep through the mud to the city. As they passed the small hootches along the river, Phil saw families fishing together. Their wooden boats were pointy-ended, their shiny varnished surfaces painted a garish red or a neon blue. From time to time little children would wave up at them from their woven bamboo boats, basketfuls of happy faces under their *non las*, the hats that symbolized a race of people for generations. The Americans waved back as they crossed the bridges that through the grace of God, had not collapsed during the monsoons. The beauty of the place inspired Phil in his stoned state to reach for a word he had learned in his 18th Century Brit Lit class. Bucolic- that was it. The scenery was bucolic. It seemed impossible to him that less than a year ago he had spent his days reading poetry and studying history and philosophy.

A young mother walked hand-in-hand with a toddler and an infant slung over her back in a crude contraption that reminded Phil of the papooses he had seen in Westerns. The child and mother smiled up at the team and waved shyly. Each one waved back except the driver. "Don't be such assholes," Dietrich growled. "Remember, the VC come in every size. They prey on the unaware and unprepared."

Dietrich's men regarded him as a true army hard ass, through and through. He had come into country at the same time that a replacement battalion commander, Major John Taylor, had arrived at their FSB and immediately changed its name to Fire Base Danger. It had been Taylor who selected the new title for their unit: The Hardcore Battalion. And Dietrich loved this leader; during the team's night ambushes, he demanded his new commandant's brand of military courtesy be exercised in the field, no matter how surreptitious the operation. A greeting, often whispered in the night, had to accompany each salute. "Hardcore Recondo, Sir!" they would say, straining to be heard.

And Dietrich would robustly respond, "No fucking SLACK!" Phil could tell how thrilled the sergeant was each time he had the opportunity to use the retort. Now he brought this same hardcore attitude with him as he drove the Jeep into My Lo for what was supposed to be a much needed and deserved day of relaxation for him and his men.

As they got closer to the city, motor scooters, bicycles, military vehicles, and donkey-drawn carts, congested the roadway. The crude river hootches and shops on the waterfront were intermingled with the classical remnants of French colonial architecture. They drove past dazzling public gardens, a racetrack, large athletic fields.

"What the hell is that place?' Graziano asked, as they passed an astonishing mansion surrounded by a five-foot high stone wall, which had been pockmarked by bullets. Barbed wire and guards bordered it.

"It's the province chief's residence," Sid, who had served in Vietnam longer than any of them, answered.

Phil could hear a band playing American tunes, not rock and roll, but Sousa type stuff. Still stoned, his stomach growled as he smelled the food ripening on the sidewalk in front of the dozens of merchants' shops in the market they were approaching. He saw children squatting, sharing huge bowls of noodles. The delicious aroma of meat cooking rose from crudely crafted smokers and makeshift clay ovens. Weird looking fruits and vegetables in wooden bins lined the streets. In other stalls, silken articles of clothing and straw hats were being tried on by civilians and military alike.

When traffic came to a dead stop, Phil turned to his right and saw a little girl selling flowers from a ramshackle hut. As he stared at her, he realized that she was probably older than he had first thought. Twelve, maybe thirteen. At home, kids her age were probably sitting in their junior high classrooms, screwing around, enjoying their lives. The girl seemed to feel his gaze. She turned toward the Jeep and smiled at him.

"Flowers for your girl, soldier," she shouted in an English far better than his own version of Vietnamese. Buckets of colorful daisies, orchids, irises, and other exotic flora Phil could not name surrounded her. She wore a red sash tied around her woven hat and a white orchid inside the makeshift band. All in one moment, Phil was charmed by her and then sickened by the realization that she reminded him of the dozens of little girls he had seen, alive and then dead in the hamlets where the infantrymen did their night work. Next to flower girl's hootch was a fishmonger. The scent given off by the various catches-of-the-day, as they began to putrefy in the blazing sun, made him queasy. He had smelled something reminiscent of this on their night sweep activities. Phil broke out in a sweat and resolved to get higher as soon as it became possible.

Traffic started moving once again, and Dietrich made the next right turn and parked near the province chief's palace. The fire team walked back toward the market together. The hustle and bustle and the myriad colors of the place reminded Phil of the few trips he had taken to New York City, where down almost every block in the summertime, a street fair could be found. The difference was, however, on closer inspection, almost every person they passed, no matter what their station in this crazy life was, seemed to be armed. Amidst the crowd strode US military, ARVN personnel, civilians, and students, distinguished by their traditional garments: long, white *ao dais* and *non las*. Although they looked much younger, Phil knew they were close to him in age. He wondered how they could focus on their studies while their country was being decimated.

"Hey, Hippie, this is your kind of shopping, right?" Kopliner, who preferred booze, laughed as they passed the rows of cannabis stands. Because it was used as an ingredient in Vietnamese recipes, and it also grew wild throughout the land, it was available to anyone who had the cash.

Phil smiled his agreement and stopped and bought an ounce of Black. He and Kopliner caught up with the rest of the guys as they headed toward the back of the large bandstand that had been set up for the celebration. They staked out a spot to hold their own little party where they could get smoked up and pass around the whiskey Sid had bought at the brothel he liked to frequent here in My Tho.

These duty-free hours passed quickly for the group. They could hardly believe that the sun was setting, but the party in the streets kept raging on. A bong had appeared out of nowhere it seemed, and Phil and Graziano, as they sat on overturned wooden crates, were hitting it hard. Phil watched as Kopliner puked behind a tree. A new band was on the stage. They were actually doing a decent rendition of the Stones' *Satisfaction*. Phil closed his eyes. He could have been at a keg party at school, Leigh Ann by his side.

He sang along with the band. "*And I try, and I try! I can't get no! I can't get no...*" Suddenly he realized that the chorus was being punctuated with screams. He opened his eyes, and through the quickly falling dusk, he saw two Marines holding on to the wrists of a little girl who was walking between them.

The three hurriedly crossed the shadowy alleyway that was about fifty feet in front of his unit's impromptu party. Phil jumped to his feet. He squinted so that he could better focus. In spite of the fading light, Phil recognized the girl. Were they dragging her? He stood on his tiptoes and tried to catch sight of her hat with the red sash, but it had disappeared in the midst of the chaotic throng.

Phil started to run in the direction of where he had last seen the three of them. A rush of adrenaline overpowered his high. He pushed through the mob of revelers, military and civilian, the red sash, an illusive beacon. Through narrow lanes and blockades of humans, he ran. In the recurring nightmares that would haunt him for years to come, the pursuit went on for what seemed like hours. In reality, he lost sight of the hat and the girl within minutes.

In spite of this, he kept running. He ran, even as he heard Dietrich and Kopliner shouting his name from behind. Minutes passed and he slowed down, so winded he struggled to get a breath. Finally, they caught up to him. Kopliner passed him and then jumped out in front of Phil, walking backwards so that he could make eye contact with his crazy buddy. "Hippie, what the hell are you doing?"

"The little kid from the flower stand. Two marines were dragging her and she was screaming..." He panted, and kept moving forward, zigging and zagging in between vacant market stands, further and further away from the celebration.

"Perrero!" his commanding officer barked from behind him. "I've told you before! Mind your own goddamned business! You're going to wind up with a bullet in your head, and it won't be the VC who do it!"

Phil forced himself to take longer strides so he could avoid interference from Dietrich and Kopliner. He willed his forward momentum to become a jogging pace, and then he stepped on something. He turned around and walked back to the spot where he had felt the object under his boot. He stared down at something on the dirt path. The smashed orchid lay beside the hat. Phil began to run.

Screams filled the night again; now the girl's shrieks were joined by the desperate shouts of a woman. As Phil ran toward the terrifying sounds, he saw a young woman standing in front of a dilapidated river hut. She wailed and shouted and tore at her hair as she paced in front of the shanty. When she saw Phil, she pointed at the doorway. Phil pushed the door open and went inside, his weapon drawn. On the floor lay the little girl, her white silk *ao dai* pushed up to her waist, the blood-soaked pantaloons around her ankles. Her eyes were open and staring, her throat slit.

Darkness, darkness, be my blanket, cover me with the endless night
Take away the pain of knowing, fill the emptiness of fright

That had been two weeks ago. His team had been on the Fire Base ever since, and there had been no night sweeps in that time. Now, as they crept toward the intact hootch on the edge of the orchard, Phil's nausea could not be contained. He ran to a strand of burned trees and retched.

He had been sick or high or both throughout his three months here. He had even shot up two or three times since the death of the flower girl. It had been the most liberating high; for a while he could forget about all the brutality and misery he had seen. This night was going to be different, though. He was straight and he was determined. He would not bear witness to any more slaughter; he had resolved after the My Tho horror that he would not stand for anymore.

Phil wiped his mouth with his handkerchief and joined his team as they made a ring around the solitary hut.

Dietrich shouted at the doorway in crude Vietnamese, "Is anyone in there? U.S. Army!" Nothing. "Come out now, or you will burn!" Graziano swung the flamethrower off of his back. Dietrich shouted again, "Come out now, or you will burn."

There was no response. Dietrich signaled to Graz. He put the M-2 to his hip, aimed it at the hut, and fired. The rest of them stood with their weapons at the ready, as the gas hissed and the flames shot out of the device that Graziano wielded. It was like killing cockroaches, Dietrich had explained to them on similar details, and that's why he had nicknamed Graz The Exterminator.

As the flames consumed the crude structure that had been a home hours before, the men heard a stirring inside, followed by screams. Phil realized as he listened to those cries that he would die here tonight.

And then the chaos started, as it always did. First, a woman streaked out from the hootch brandishing a long knife at the fire team. She slashed at the air with the weapon as she tried to break through the parameter of soldiers. Dietrich interceded and smashed her in the mouth with the butt of his rifle. "Son of a bitch!" he shouted.

As she fell to the ground, six children ran out of the hut, including a young boy carrying a toddler. They all stopped when they saw their mother, her bleeding face spotlighted in the flames from their burning home. High, sweet voices, the most broken sound Phil had ever heard, cried, "Ma', ma'," most likely the first word the children had learned and spoken. At its orginal utterance, they had probably been surrounded by people who loved them and whose approval and appreciation they saw reflected back at them when they spoke it. Phil knew that feeling; his mother had made him feel loved and accepted, always.

He looked around at his team and saw them through the terrified children's eyes. He stood in their shoes. The audience tonight who heard their cries of "Ma', ma'!" were not adoring family, but large men in monster costumes.

Dietrich screamed, "Hold..." but the point man's words did not register as a command to the veteran fighter, Sid. He had already raised his weapon and aimed it at the baby's head. Phil lunged toward Pouthier, a father himself, who seemed not to understand that these were *people* at his mercy. After three tours of duty, Sid did not see humans before him; he had been trained to think they were a sub-species or an alien type of vermin, and he believed it. Phil grabbed at Sid's powerful arm, and was shrugged off like a fly.

Resolute, Phil raised his rifle and aimed it at Sid's head. And then, Kopliner, fucking Kopliner, clutched him in a chokehold from behind, and in those crucial seconds, Phil went limp.

Sid fired. And kept on firing. He paused. He laid his M-16 on the ground and took a pistol out of his holster. He put it up to the mother's temple and pulled the trigger.

Freedom Bird. That was what they called the plane that carried him to the base in Hawaii where Phil would spend the next three years, a twenty-one year old with a heroin habit and crippling PTSD.

He opened the magazine on his lap. It was the issue of *Tour 365*, the one that all who were ending a tour of duty in Vietnam received. In the front of this issue was a letter from the Commanding General, a personalized message to Phil and his comrades.

"Your tour of duty with the United States Army, Vietnam, is ended. May your trip home and reunion with family and friends be the pleasant, happy occasion you have anticipated...

As veterans of this war, you can now look back with perspective on your experiences and know the trying and difficult tasks inherent in fighting to protect the freedom of peace-loving people against Communist invaders. You know of the local Viet Cong terrorists who kill and maim their own neighbors, and appreciate the terror and destruction they spread. Having served here, you understand better than many of our countrymen the meaning of aggression against South Vietnam.

Many of you have worked with people in the hamlet improvement and pacification programs and been looked upon as a teacher and builder, as well as a fighter.

People at home will want to hear your story of the war. Tell it...

I extend my sincere appreciation for your help in accomplishing our task in Vietnam, and my thanks for a job well done. Good luck in the future."

Creighton w. Abrams
General, United States Army
Commanding

Chapter Five — "You're Not Okay"

"You embarrassed me tonight, but more importantly, you embarrassed *yourself.*" Peter quietly but intently listed the particulars of the offenses Leigh Ann had most recently perpetrated. It was conceivable that to an outsider, the handsome middle-aged man might appear calm, almost tranquil as he spoke to his wife. But she knew very well that Peter's outward composure belied the extreme hostility he felt. If this hypothetical outsider happened to look more closely at her husband, said stranger might notice, as his wife most certainly did, that the tall man's hands were balled into fists.

Whenever Peter's explanations went on for a long time, his voice, though still in that same gentle register, might tremble momentarily and betray him. If the couple happened to be out in public during one of these "discussions", anyone walking by might observe their intimate posture and the sincerity on Peter's face and think, "Wow! That guy is really into his woman..."

But Leigh Ann, of course, knew what casual observers did not. He was furious with her once again.

In their first couple of years together, she would try to defend herself against his accusations. But after the kids were born, she could fake just the right amount of attentiveness, a signal from the outset that she was conceding to his opinions of her. Her greatest wish throughout every one of his quiet rants was for it to be over as quickly as possible. She knew how to play her role if she wanted to achieve this goal. She did not fight back. She offered no excuses or defenses. Instead, she would gradually assume a submissive posture, sitting in the passenger seat of the car, a booth in one of the greasy diners he loved, at their kitchen table, wherever they might be, with her head down and her eyes cast on a nearby object. Occasionally, when she had the strength, she would actually focus on what he was saying and try to see her imperfect self from his "objective" point of view. During these episodes, she would look at him directly and nod in agreement. He would lecture her until he felt satisfied with his analysis of the infractions she had committed. Eventually, thank God, he ran out of things to say, and the monologue was over.

Most women would not have put up with their mates' frequent criticisms and judgments of their behavior, their very character. Other women might have held a grudge. But Leigh Ann prided herself on her ability to move on. She had the capacity to see each day following one of Peter's tirades as a fresh start. If she smoked enough weed, she could actually erase the memory of his most recent lecture. Survivor's endurance, that's what she had. She counted this trait as a strength. She could thank her mother for offering her plenty of practice with this strategy during childhood and adolescence.

Leigh Ann and Peter had met at a party given by her graduate program director Jim Courts and his wife Angie at their home in Albany. It was a mixer for the twenty new students who had earned places in the MA program that Jim had designed and launched through SUNY a couple of years before. Leigh Ann was thrilled to have been accepted and to have won a fellowship that included a small living stipend. Peter Forbes was an alum of the program, but he had recently left the world of college teaching behind. He was working on his doctorate in higher ed administration at SUNY Albany. Jim had invited him that day because Peter was an impressive young man, the kind of person you would like to introduce to your new batch of graduate students and say, "Hey, this guy went through the program you've been accepted to... look how well he's doing."

Peter was very blond with eyes that were a deep blue. He bore a resemblance to the John Voigt of that day, although he was lankier and had sharper features. He was not Leigh Ann's preferred physical type at all, really. She recognized that he was handsome in a pressed-jeans-and-blazer kind of way. He was one of those tall people who gave the impression of being even taller than he actually was because he only occasionally looked at you directly when he spoke. Most of the time his eyes targeted something just above your head, as if he were really carrying on a conversation with the invisible person who had three inches on you. His aloofness was one of the things that attracted a certain type of woman. That cool exterior offered a challenge to that kind of female. There must be a beating heart somewhere that woman would say to herself, and I must find it! Leigh Ann did not believe that she was that type of woman.

At their first meeting, he had walked into the room with a beautiful blond, so similar to him physically, they could have been siblings. "Hey, Leigh Ann, come over here. I want you to meet someone," Jim called to her.

Wine glass in hand, she walked over to the small circle that had gathered around Jim and the striking couple. "Peter Forbes, meet Leigh Ann Fray, a SUNY grad like yourself, and one of the program's most promising candidates." As they shook hands, the tall guy looked down at her and smiled politely. She realized suddenly that she recognized him from a class they had taken together when she was a freshman. Dr. Wilson's Myths and Legends. They had never spoken back then. He was a senior and well-aware of his superiority in that classroom and everywhere else on the planet, she had realized, as she looked at the back of his blond head for a semester.

"Nice to meet you, Leigh Ann. This is my fiancé, Margo." She shook hands with the blond whose height almost equaled that of her husband-to-be. The woman looked exquisitely Scandinavian, and Leigh Ann would not have been surprised if someone had told her that Margo was an Olympian, or maybe a swimsuit model. Or both.

75

"Hello," she said to Leigh Ann. "Peter, we're going to have to get going soon," the woman said. "I'll grab our coats. Nice to have met you, Luanne. Good luck with the program."

Leigh Ann spoke to the back of the head of the retreating Margo. "*Leigh Ann*, it's Leigh Ann..."

"Sorry about that," he said. Mr. Nose- In -The- Air actually chuckled as he added, "Details are not her strong suit. Listen, here's my number. If you have any questions about the program or the city, don't hesitate to call." Peter was making an effort to sound warm and sincere, but she wasn't buying it. The guy and his look-alike girlfriend were so obviously cold fish.

"Thanks," she said as Peter Forbes turned and walked away.

The next time she saw him was in a record store in Buffalo months later. She was completing her internship, teaching two classes at Erie Community College and putting the finishing touches on her master's thesis. Buffalo in the '70's was a great place to be young. The music scene and the night life, the experimental theater at Studio Arena, the concerts at Kleinhans, the many great bookstores, and the Albright Knox; it was a city whose vibrancy ran a close second to

New York, scaled down, of course. But Buffalo was more affordable and safer, much safer. Leigh Ann was loving her life in this city.

"Hey, I know you," she said, as she looked across the record bins at the man standing opposite her.

Peter looked up at her from the albums he had been searching through and said, "Luanne, right?" He laughed at her open-mouthed consternation and said, "*Leigh Ann* Fray, can you not take a joke?"

"Very funny. Is the lovely Margaret with you tonight?" She had to admit, she was flattered that he had remembered her at all.

"Ha! Touché," he said and grinned. Wait, was that a dimple she was seeing on this large Aryan face? "No," he said, suddenly sober. "The beautiful Margo dumped me for one of my professors. How's that for incestuous choices?"

"Oh. I'm sorry," she said, trying to sound like she meant it. But his reference to incest made her smile, since she had thought of them as twins when they had met at Jim's party.

"Yeah. Thanks, but it was more than likely inevitable. Better now than later, right?" He returned her smile and said, "So I had heard that Jim Court's prize teacher was in Buffalo. How do you like it?"

"Love it!" she said. "And what about you? What are you doing here?"

"Well, for one thing, I grew up here. I love Western New York, and I've always wanted to get back to it, so I'm finishing my doctorate at UB. After Margot gave me the shaft, I decided to get the hell out of Albany. Get back to my roots."

He looked at the album she was holding. "Robert Lockwood, Jr., huh? You're brilliant *and* you're a blues fan? I may have to take you to Nietzsche's tonight. There's a great group playing there all weekend." He looked at his watch. "First set starts at 11. What do you think?"

Leigh Ann moved in with him that summer. Years later, she would realize that the happiest times in their relationship were shared in that duplex on Shreck Avenue in Buffalo. They cooked together or ate take-out in the small galley kitchen each night. He would drink a beer or open a bottle of wine with dinner; she sometimes rolled a joint and they would have great conversations late into the night about *everything*: philosophy, politics, education, books, film, art. And music. They appreciated all styles, every genre. Leigh Ann thought of their first "date" at Nietzsche's as the beginning of their sharing a mutual life-long passion. They pooled their money and bought an expensive sound system and listened to everything, often holding one another and dancing around the tiny living room.

They each brought old friends into their circle of two, and it seemed to Leigh Ann almost magical how all of these seemingly dissimilar people became friends, too. The Shreck Avenue apartment parties were the best, they all agreed. Every weekend at least ten or more friends would start at their place and then extend the night into the wee hours of the morning at the Tralf or one of the other dozen or so music clubs around the city.

Peter and Leigh Ann made love everywhere in that little apartment, often several times a day on the weekends. Soul mates, Leigh Ann thought to herself. As perfect as she thought they were for one another, she never said it out loud. She knew it would make Peter crazy to hear their relationship so tritely described.

Leigh Ann delivered her thesis in November, and in January, she and Peter moved to Kingston. She had been offered a position as an associate professor of English at Vassar, and Peter had gotten an administrative internship at Duchess Community College. They were sad to have to leave Buffalo, but Leigh Ann was eager to begin her professional life in this beautiful part of the state. The Hudson Valley reminded her so much of the natural splendor of the Catskills, but with a culture that better suited her liberated spirit.

Leigh Ann and Peter drove the few miles from their apartment in Kingston to Woodstock almost every weekend. The artists' colony inspired Leigh Ann. She had been journaling and writing since she was a teenager, and while she was in grad school she had actually had two of her essays published in small monographs. But in her new full-time teaching role, she had little time to write. The young woman from working class parents had to, first and foremost, make a living. Leigh Ann the writer would have to take a back seat to Leigh Ann the teacher, who actually earned a regular paycheck.

Most of the residents of Woodstock, however, had rejected materialism for the sake of creativity, and living this close to this cultural enclave satisfied Leigh Ann's need for artistic stimulation. She and Peter would walk around the small town and browse through books in The Golden Notebook, or explore the many sculptors' studios; they especially loved the impromptu concerts in the various bars. On any given Saturday, they could see The Band or sometimes Levon Helm playing solo.

Leigh Ann felt blessed to be starting her professorial career at Vassar. Almost every one of her new colleagues was from the same student-centered school of thought as she. Their older, more traditional department chair was willing to indulge these new professors in their pursuit to engage these twentieth century learners. Leigh Ann had never worked harder in her life as she did those first few years in the classroom. Staying one step ahead of the students in her composition and literary criticism classes took hours of exertion, but she had never felt more mentally stimulated and exhilarated.

On the other hand, Peter said that he was just biding his time at Duchess until his dream job at a *real* university came along. He told her that his talents were being wasted here, and he made it clear that he wanted to get back to Western New York as soon as they could. Leigh Ann said nothing, hoping that somehow fate would intercede on her behalf, and that they would stay in the Hudson Valley forever.

They were engaged that summer. Her parents approved of their "flighty" daughter's choice, although Leigh Ann was not convinced that her father felt entirely comfortable around Peter. She consoled herself with the knowledge that her favorite parent had never fully accepted anyone she had dated in the past.

On a sunny day in September, Peter and Leigh Ann walked from her parents' house to the small town hall in Sidney. At the end of the five minute ceremony, with just the court cop as a witness, the justice of the peace, who had doubled as a substitute teacher during her high school years, pronounced them man and wife. Mr. Richter, who the kids had called "Stricter Richter", seemed incredulous when Leigh Ann told him she was keeping her surname. It was the early seventies in a small town in the Northeast, and the generation gap was blatant. "Okay," he said, still shaking his head in bewilderment, "then sign right here, *Ms. Fray.*"

Because they were paying for it themselves, the reception was modest, but exactly reflected their tastes and personalities. It was held in a community park in the Catskills amidst the brilliant late September foliage. Peter had hired their favorite band from Buffalo. Everyone, the Fray and the Forbes families, along with the many friends Leigh Ann and Peter had collected in their two years together, drank wine and beer and danced in the grass until sundown. Peter's father had presented them with a modest check when they had gotten engaged, and they used a portion of it to hire a photographer, an art student at Delhi who had bought himself a nice camera when he had served in the army in Germany. Years later, Leigh Ann loved showing this album to her small children. Lilly and David wanted to know who each and every person was and what was going on in each picture.

The fights began shortly after their wedding. Almost always, the arguments were about the same thing: Leigh Ann's carelessness, failures, and missteps. Sometimes Peter could not wait to get home to give her a full accounting of them, and the squabble would start in a public place. But more often they would take place when they would return home, first to their apartments and later to their various houses in the Hudson Valley, or once they had relocated to Western New York, to their beautiful old home in Ellicottville.

It might be a few short hours after her offense, when cold anger would darken his voice, or perhaps the next morning, when his tone was that of the erudite college administrator. He would outline her unpleasant behavior during a dinner party with his colleagues, a night out with his parents in Buffalo, a reunion with friends over a beer and wings. Peter wanted his wife to gain some objective perspective about her failings, so together they attended groups and read books designed to help her see more clearly the error of her ways. Even in settings where she was trying to learn from her "mistakes," Peter observed her shortcomings. During the time early on in their marriage when they belonged to a Transactional Analysis group, and then in their marriage therapy sessions in the 80's, all the way into the family counseling sessions Peter arranged when David began acting out, her husband could find fault with her behavior and enumerate for her the reasons for his disappointment with her.

"Why do you feel the need to make everyone in the room like you? It's childish and embarrassing. Why can't you get over the fact that your mother never liked you much and your father overcompensated for that? It's not normal for an adult woman to need that much attention. Maybe you shouldn't smoke so much weed before we go out and then chase it with a gin and tonic or two. Are you taking nothing out of TA (the 70's), therapy, (the 80's) counseling (the 90's)?" Leigh Ann could have scripted these lectures after a couple of years of sitting in silence as he reprimanded her. He was very persuasive, she had to admit. And as the years passed, she found that she often agreed with his assessment of her.

By the time the kids had reached their early teens, Peter was miserable most of the time, although by now he had uprooted them and brought them back to his beloved Western New York. He criticized everything she did or did not do. "You smoke too much weed. You don't really clean deeper than the surface, do you? Why are you still dressing like it's the 60's? You didn't pay that bill on time. Did you ever think about befriending some people whom you *haven't* known for decades? You let David get away with too much. You don't praise Lilly enough." The judgments went beyond the scope of her personal flaws; he would often criticize her friends, her colleagues, her teaching methods, the column she had started to write for the local paper. And by the time he had taken a new position as dean of students at a private college in Buffalo, their love making was something she initiated or it did not happen. His forty-minute commute seemed to leave Peter physically exhausted and disinterested.

Leigh Ann did not confide in her friends about Peter's belittling of her, nor did she share any of it in their family therapy sessions. She chose to believe that their kids were not aware of their problems, nor was anyone else, for that matter. After all, what their friends, their co-workers, and the neighbors in their small community saw when they looked at Peter and Leigh Ann was an attractive, professional couple in early middle age, who were in a long-term, happy relationship. So she hoped she was right, that the kids were not conscious of their father's dissatisfaction with their mother's shortfalls. But she could see that Lilly was spending more and more time at her friends' houses; sometimes she stayed away from their home for days at a time. And Leigh Ann observed a change in their son, too, although she did not want to admit it. David's rebellious behavior was the reason they *had* to seek family counseling, according to Peter.

When Lilly left for her freshman year at Fredonia, it was just the three of them in their house in Ellicottville. David, a junior in high school, had just turned seventeen and it became obvious to Leigh Ann that her son had a much more realistic picture of his parents' marriage than anyone else in their lives. He had a seething contempt for his father, barely veiled. When he witnessed another of his father's "lectures," he readily became his mother's protector and deflected Peter's criticisms of Leigh Ann, purposely redirecting his father's attention to himself. The difference between David and his mother was that the angry teen *would* fight back. He was his father's son when it came to being able to make a cogent, passionate argument.

During David's final year at home, the tension between his father and him was palpable. Their son was a talented guitarist and vocalist in a punk pop band. The group was popular throughout the region, and his grades in his senior year were, while not entirely reflective of his ability, the best they had been so far in his high school career. In spite of these accomplishments, when David was out of the house, at band practice or hanging out with friends, Leigh Ann would have to listen to Peter's long tirades about their son's many failures. When he came home, sometimes under the influence of some substance, father and son would engage in loud, long arguments.

It was Peter who made an appointment with a family counselor in Buffalo, since Ellicottville was such a tiny community and word would certainly get out that all was not Waltonesque in the Forbes-Fray household. He assured Leigh Ann that the eighty minute round trip commute would be worth it. They could use the time in the car to talk with their son about his "problems." The three of them could go out for a nice meal in the city every couple of weeks; they could show their son the places they had loved so many years ago. Leigh Ann had conceded and pretended to be convinced that the bimonthly ordeal might improve their family dynamic.

"He's a dick!" was David's go-to line when the counselor asked what he saw as the problem in their family. Peter stared at his son's pointing finger, bewildered.

One night, shortly before David's graduation, he did not come home by his midnight curfew. At one AM, Leigh Ann lay in bed, while her husband angrily paced back and forth in the living room. She dreaded the scene that would take place. David was not like her; he wouldn't tolerate his father's demanding questions or scathing criticisms. Just then, she heard her son's key in the door and she sat up in bed.

"Where have you been?" she heard her husband ask. His controlled tone did not mask his anger. It was a veneer that Leigh Ann, after years of experiencing it, did not believe.

She listened harder for her son's reply and heard, "something, something... band practice..." and then a sickening crash and her son's shout.

"You fucking fascist! Don't put your hands on me!" Leigh Ann jumped out of bed and ran to the front of the house.

"Just because Mom puts up with your shit..." she watched as Peter clenched the collar of David's leather jacket in both hands. Her son was pinned to the wall, and Peter's face was inches from his. "Let me go, you bastard!" he said, as his knee connected with his father's testicles.

Leigh Ann watched as her husband doubled over in pain. David escaped out the front door, slamming it hard. "Run, son, run," she prayed in silence.

"Call the cops! Now, Leigh Ann!" He was still bent over and trying to catch his breath.

"No," she said.

When he could finally stand, the argument began, and this time, both of them were invested in it.

"What do you mean, no? The little bastard is out of control. He attacked me!" She saw the spit fly as he shouted.

"You cornered him. He felt trapped. You gave him no choice!" She was shrieking, she knew, but she could not stop herself.

"You've lost your mind, Leigh Ann." He walked to the desk and picked up the phone.

Her body reacted before she knew what she was doing. He had crossed a line, finally. The insults, criticisms, judgments of her, she could tolerate. But the primal urge to protect that kid was invincible. The mothers who have moved cars off of their children with their super strength would understand how Leigh Ann Fray dared to take her husband on that night. She picked up the heavy steel letter opener off the desk and threw it at the hand that held the phone receiver.

"Fuck!" Peter screamed, all vestiges of his signature self-control stripped away. The phone clattered onto the desk.

"We do not call the cops on our kids! Ever! Do you understand me?" She recognized the influence of Peter's incessant disapproval in the tone of her own voice.

"Three fractured phalanges," the young doctor in the Buffalo ER pronounced as he looked at Peter's x-ray. Her husband had insisted she drive to the city so that the news would not travel all over Ellicottville. "We'll get those splinted and send you on your way with a prescription that should help with the pain, Mr. Forbes."

On the trip back home, as the sun began to rise, Leigh Ann agreed with Peter that the three of them had to see the family counselor immediately. The next day, Dr. Girard set up an appointment to have David tested. When the results were back, they supported the therapist's diagnosis. The condition was called "oppositional defiance disorder," and this label, indicative of emotional instability, and ascribed to his angry son, seemed to placate Peter.

Her husband was uncharacteristically silent during most of that summer. Leigh Ann told herself that perhaps this was the beginning of a new chapter for them. After all, they had been together for years and had weathered some bad times in the past. Now that the kids were both going to be out of the house, she told herself, they would have the opportunity to renew their relationship.

That fall, with David joining Lilly at Fredonia, Peter did seem more at peace. His assessments of her were infrequent and dispassionate. They became good roommates, although Leigh Ann had every intention of building on this new tranquility. She was simply waiting for the right time to become Peter's lover again.

On a Saturday morning following a comfortable evening they had shared with two other couples, friends of theirs for years, Leigh Ann awoke alone in the big bed. She looked at the clock. Oh, my God... 10:45! "Peter? Why didn't you wake me?" she called into the empty space. She put on her robe and slippers and gently pushed two cats out of her way. "Peter?"

She walked into the kitchen and looked around. Clean coffee pot, no dishes in the sink. She looked out the window into the garden. He was not there. Something that did not belong on the old farmhouse table caught her eye. It was a yellow post-it note. Leigh Ann's hands started to tingle and she felt the fine hairs on the back of her neck bristle. She grabbed her glasses from her purse that lay on the counter and walked back to the table.

In his precise cursive was Peter's last pronouncement of her. "Leigh Ann, You made a choice last spring, and you chose David. It was a bad choice. I am through. I will be staying with my parents if any emergencies should arise. Get an attorney. I already have one."

Chapter Six — What Dreams

With her back to the little girl, the woman furiously pulls clothing off hangers in the closet, balls up blouses, skirts, slacks, and jams each article into a black garbage bag. She opens the dresser drawers and does the same with socks, underwear, nightgowns. Then she kneels down on the closet floor and pulls out several pairs of shoes. There is a frantic rhythm to each movement, as if she is in fear for her life. She is breathing very hard and grunting with every effort. The little girl follows the woman step for step all around the small bedroom. Frantic for the woman's attention, the little girl puts herself in the midst of her path, but she turns away from the child. The girl runs behind the figure. She reaches out and tugs on the hem of the woman's black sweater. The woman does not seem to be aware of the child at all.

The little girl watches as the woman places the two overflowing garbage bags on the floor. Her desperation to be recognized is turning into panic. The child has been trying to speak this whole time, but her voice is frozen. With tremendous effort, she is finally able to call out. "Mama!" The sound is rusty, grating. The woman turns around at last and kneels down in front of the girl. She reaches her arms out to her.

The child is thrilled to at last have her presence acknowledged. She runs toward the figure faster than she has ever run, smiling, with her eyes half closed. When she reaches the woman, the girl opens her eyes. Her smile vanishes as she stares into nothingness.

She recoils from the featureless countenance. It is as if eyes, nose, mouth, cheekbones, forehead, chin, all have been erased. She feels the arms of the woman wrap around her waist, tightening like a snake. The little girl struggles until she frees herself from the constraint. She wants to run from the faceless horror, but when she tries to take a step, she is frozen by a familiar panic.

A buzzing sounds in Charlotte's ear. She is awakened by the hum that always precedes the Voice. She opens her eyes to the total darkness of her bedroom. She has been crying in her sleep, and she is soaked in sweat. "Call her," the Voice instructs.

She sits up and takes her phone from the table next to the bed. Flipping it open, she pushes one button on the keypad. Within seconds the connection is made and in her sleep-filled voice Charlotte croaks, "Hey, Leigh Ann, it's me. So I had this horrible dream, and I wanted to talk to you about it. Give me a call when you can."

"Text her. She can't ignore that," the Voice says.

She types, *Hey, which act is it where Hamlet says something about "What dreams may come?*

The Voice says, "You're running out of time. That guy who's been looking for her will take her away from you. Did you really think she would be discouraged by your "Cool Hunter" advice in the Ellicottville Courier? Maybe she hasn't even read those comments." Charlotte had thoughtfully responded to Leigh Ann's column about the man and his email. But the Voice was not impressed by her efforts.

"Make a plan, Charlotte. Execute it," the Voice says.

Charlotte climbs out of her bed and pulls a backpack from her closet. Crossing the room, she opens her desk drawer and pulls out a stack of papers clipped together with a fat metal clamp. She shoves this into the bottom of the bag.

"Call her again." The Voice has a certainty that cannot be denied.

"Hey, Leigh Ann. It's me again. Still trying to get over that dream. Hope you're okay."

She hangs up again and the Voice reassures her, "You're special to Leigh Ann. You are more than her student, anyone can see that. You have to be with her, Charlotte, always. Without her, you're nothing. "

The Voice is right, she knows. Charlotte opens her closet and grabs sweaters, shirts, jeans, enough for three days. A shiver runs up her spine and the nightmare washes back over her as she realizes that she, like the creature in her dream, is furiously packing. From her dresser she pulls out underwear, socks, sweats. She shoves all into the backpack.

"But just in case, get the gun," the Voice says.

The house is quiet. The kids and her father have been asleep for hours. She opens her door and tiptoes across the hallway to her father's room. Carefully, she opens his door and is relieved to see that he is alone in the bed. Thankfully, there is no door on his closet. She reaches up, and from the shelf she takes the .38 and a box of ammunition.

She quietly reenters her bedroom and packs the gun and extra rounds. Then she shoves the bag into the back of her closet.

"And when you go into work, ask for extra shifts. You're going to need the money to travel across country. Google Lilly's and David's addresses, so you can put them into the GPS." The Voice always has her back.

"Text her," it says now.

The buzzing that accompanies the Voice is diminishing. Charlotte knows that it will soon be silent.

Good night, Leigh Ann, she texts, *and thank you for being such a good friend.*

Chapter Seven — R & R

He hears the buzz of a plane's engine overhead. The sun is shining brightly. Phil is smiling as he opens the door to the long, low building. He is certain that she will be here and that she will be so happy that he came. He walks through one beaded curtain and then another, the only barrier between each of the small spaces in the dilapidated building. As he gets closer to the room where he knows she will be, he hears the girl's quiet weeping.

He quickens his pace, following the sound of her crying. She is sitting in the middle of the little room on a tiny cot, staring straight ahead. When she sees Phil, she stops crying and with the backs of her hands, she wipes the tears from her face. A stranger, a Marine, sits next to her. Phil is reaching for his revolver just as the Marine pulls the girl's head back by her long dark hair; her throat is perfectly exposed for the work of the long blade that he holds in his right hand. The executioner looks from the flower girl to Phil and back. He slowly draws the cutting edge across her throat. He is intent only on his work, as if he is alone in the room. Paralyzed with horror, Phil watches. He tries to move toward the two, but he is powerless. The little girl's blood spurts, splatters, and then flows. It pours down her white *ao dai*, it hits the walls, it splashes over Phil's face, and then it is rushing like a river over his feet. The last thing he sees before he closes his eyes is the white orchid next to her blood soaked hat lying on the floor.

He gasps awake and opens his eyes. Sweat runs down from the top of his scalp onto his forehead. He grabs his wristwatch off the table next to the bed. Five AM. Time doesn't really matter this week, since he doesn't have to be anywhere, but checking on the time, such a mundane action helps Phil shake off the horror of the dream. He reminds himself that he is on R&R. He has not slept through the night once in the six months since his tour of duty; so far, being away from the base has not made a difference.

Recently, he has been talking to the base shrink in vague terms, anyway, about the nightmares. When he is asked, Phil answers yes, they are affecting the way he performs his clerical duties on base. He is exhausted and muddled all day.

"I've been reading a study about a method being used stateside that seems to be helping people who have sleep interruption because of recurring dreams. Kids who have experienced trauma of some sort, Korean vets, and guys in your situation are having some success with it," the shrink had told Phil. " You've told me how much you'd like to return to being the guy you were before the war."

"You mean, before I turned into a zombie? " Phil was not exaggerating. The emptiness that had invaded his head and heart crowded out any emotion. The shrink had told Phil that the nightmares and insomnia following them were most likely responsible for this apathy.

"With this method you don't need drugs or a psychiatrist to facilitate it. Waikiki might be a good place for you to try it out."

As the shrink had explained it to him, Phil thought the technique made sense. It might actually help him eradicate these nightmares, unlike the talk- talk-talking done in group therapy, or in his solo sessions with the psychiatrist. The method was called Imagery Rehearsal Therapy. What you were supposed to do was concentrate on one recurring nightmare and "rewrite" it during the daytime. Change some of the disturbing details, and rehearse the new version a few times while you went about your business in the light of day. Then when you fell asleep, because you had practiced visualizing it the way you wanted it, the idea was that your subconscious would carry out the new version of the dream, or at least weaken the virulence of the original.

Since leaving the jungle, Phil had had several persistent nightmares; the scenarios were different, but they all ended the same. In each one, he would come so close to saving someone from harm; an old Vietnamese lady, a guy from his fire team, a peasant child, but ultimately, he would be strangled by that bizarre paralysis, and he would awaken from the dream to an overwhelming and unrelenting sense of shame and then a numbness that replaced sleep.

So here he was at the beach, and for the third night in a row, the shrink's strategy had not helped him. When he had arrived on Sunday and every day since, he had mindfully reconstructed his dream of the little girl in My Tho. He went over and over the new details and emotions that he hoped would override the terrifying ones.

In his daytime version, her bright red hat band was his reliable compass, and he stayed close behind the Marines as they fled through the back streets of the city with the flower girl between them. The three entered a small hootch with Phil following right on their heels. He burst into the room where the three of them were, catching the men off guard. He grabbed one of them and pummeled him, alternating the target of the blows between the man's face and chest until he fell to the dirt floor. He turned to the other guy who held the girl tightly by the shoulders. Phil reached for his revolver, and the Marine let the girl go. Then he watched as the two men fled. A woman, just a bit older than him, came through the doorway, and Phil left the small hut as mother and child embraced. With this replacement dream supplanting the brutal truth, Phil thought he might be able to live with himself again.

But so far, the strategy has not worked; in fact, it has backfired. Each night, it seems as though the nightmares are much more vivid and terrifying than they had been. The pall they cast over him lasts far into the day. In the afternoon he walks down to the beach with a blanket and a book, which he never opens. He sits on the white sand visualizing again his alternative dream of the flower girl. A few tourists walk by, some couples hand in hand, and it seems like they are staring at him, like they understand who he has become. In the daytime, Phil wears his dishonor like a brand, and as he sleeps, his mind replays his cowardliness.

Now, halfway through his leave, Phil swings his legs over the side of the bed and onto the floor. He pulls on his clothes and walks into the tiny cottage kitchen and looks out the window at the Pacific. He could have booked a room at one of the big resort hotels, as most servicemen on R&R in Oahu did, but Phil knew a guy who had rented this little place from one of the doormen at the Ocean Reef Hotel. It is at the western end of the island, mainly away from the hustle and bustle of the tourists. Now that he is clean and sober, he needs some privacy and time to himself.

He makes some instant coffee and lights a cigarette. The air coming in through the screen door smells of salt and flowers, and the rising sun washes over Phil's face. The roar of the surf is alien to the man from northern New York State. He had been at Fort Shafter for six months, but he could have been in Kansas for all he had seen of the island. His first three months there were spent drying out from alcohol and withdrawing from the heroin he had used on a daily basis at the end of his tour of duty. When he wasn't doing his boring clerical job on base, he was attending a group therapy session or seeing the shrink one-on-one. Besides being exhausted, he was sick of base life, sick of the people, the food, sick of being sick. He was a very old man inside his twenty-one-year-old's body. This week, although he is supposed to be on a relaxing leave, he will be working on trying to get his shit together. The IRT method has not been successful, but he has another resource that Phil hopes might bring him some peace.

Carrying his coffee mug in one hand and a cardboard box under his arm, Phil pushes the screen door open. He sets the box and his coffee on the picnic table and sits down, facing the ocean. Tearing the tape off the cardboard seam, he opens the box and pulls out the familiar black bag. Phil has never been sure about its original purpose; maybe it had been a woman's purse in the '30's or '40's. It was scarred and cracked from a decade or so of dormancy followed by several years of handling that had worn its leather cover thin. Inside it were a hundred or so letters, still in their original GI envelopes, all addressed to Margaret Perrero.

As a kid, Phil had read and reread them, so much so, that years later, he could still recognize his particular favorites from their envelopes. The ones he had read over and over again were not the "mushy" ones, as he had thought of them as a kid. Back then, he was a fatherless boy, looking for a key to understanding why he had been abandoned. Years later and thousands of miles from where he had originally discovered them, he was searching these letters for a different answer. He was probing them now, looking for a kinship more significant than blood.

When his mother had found him bent over one of the letters as a nine, then a ten, then a twelve-year-old, she had asked him, "Why do you want to read those old things, Philly? That's all water under the bridge. I've always meant to pitch them." But she hadn't. She knew the letters and a few very dated photos were all her boy had of his father. When Phil had written to her a month ago and asked that she send them in her next package, she had obliged.

He unties the old cloth shoelaces that held the stack together. His father had meticulously dated each one, starting with December 12, 1942, and Phil had a vague memory of sorting through them on his bedroom floor and organizing them chronologically as a young teenager. He had asked her many times, but his mother had seemed frustratingly clueless as to exactly what her husband did or where he had served those three and a half years. All she knew is that they had been married a year and that he had been in his third year of college at Canisius in Buffalo. He was majoring in biology, and he was planning on applying to medical school, but then he had been drafted. When he came back almost four years later, he was not the same; he was never the same, his mother had said. The war had ruined his life. And hers, that is, until Phil was born.

She had listened intently as her young son read a portion of one of the earliest letters to her, hoping she would remember more details of his time in the service.

"Dear Marge,
I wanted to tell you what I've been up to lately.
I've been pretty bored until today. I was goldbricking
this afternoon and Sgt. Belden caught me. I was
strolling along the halls and he snatched me to help with
a convoy. Boy, I know I've griped before about this job I
didn't ask for, sweetheart, but I'm cured after today.
Some of those boys that go on strike in some of those
defense plants that have been in the paper lately should
have seen what I saw today. I carried one fellow to a
ward. He was paralyzed on one side and he had a body
cast and the stink and stench was awful. It was pathetic

*and no kidding it really got me and he wasn't the only
one. I'm sending you a clipping about the convoy. This
place really made copy today. We had three newspaper
articles written about us, and Life magazine is coming
next week."*

"Yeah, that's right," she told her son. "After his
basic training, he was stationed in a big army hospital in
Memphis. He was a kind of orderly, I guess you could
say. Probably because he had been a biology major when
they drafted him. I took the train down there with my
sister right before he went to Europe. When he went
over there, he drove a Jeep all over the place - great use
of his science background, huh? And then, near the end
of the war, he was captured."

That was pretty much the extent of his mother's
knowledge of Frank's war experience. Some of his
letters referred vaguely to "France," Somewhere in
Belgium," or "Somewhere in England," at the top. Up
until the time that Phil had become more interested in
girls than researching his father's whereabouts during his
time in the army, he had read about the European Front
and traced a chronological path that ended in his father's
captivity in Germany in 1945. Now, Phil, a combat
veteran himself, would reread every page with new eyes,

looking for the details that might help him face his own crippling shame and deal with it.

Once Frank Perrero had crossed the Channel, it seemed to Phil that the majority of his letters avoided any direct mention of the war and the combat he saw. Most of what his father wrote to his mother concerned their relationship, how much he missed and loved her. As far as his daily routine, he mainly talked about his social life "such as it is"- who he played cards with, what movies he saw, and what music he was listening to. As a kid, Phil had been frustrated with these descriptions of the dated and the mundane. Later, he understood that the letters written by those who served to their loved ones at home were censored. Phil was now able to read between the lines and see subtle hints of fear and dread in his father's words.

> *"Dear Marge,*
> *I cant' believe it has been about three months since I last saw you. Not quite as long as we have been separated on other occasions, but I'm wondering. Has this one affected you anymore than usual? I know it has me but I don't get the time to mope around about it. I've been very uneasy the last few days. I can't account for it but I'm tense. It's hardly possible for me to relax. It's as though I were expecting something to happen, but what I don't know. I hope that everything is alright at home. Perhaps it's the lack of mail coupled with current events*

that reacts on me so. I don't know but I do hope that you are OK. The only thing that keeps us going is the fact that those we left behind us at home are with us 100%. So if you ever get discouraged remember that little thought. For the present you shouldn't worry about my welfare because I'm comparatively safe. Of course there is always a chance of catching a cold or dying of pneumonia. Seriously dear I'm really OK and in the best spirits. I love you, perhaps that's the reason that I can contend with my lot."

His father's last letter written from the front was surprisingly detailed. The Allies were closing in on their victory, and more than likely, the censors were much less vigilant.

"Dear Marge,
There seems no end to this bloody conflict. I always had a feeling that I could participate more actively than I had up until now. Now, I am in the thick of it, Marge.
When I get home to you, I want to put these three years behind me and live our life. But there are things I don't ever want to forget about it too. Lots of guys are collecting things to bring home so they won't forget. I actually had a German helmet in France but it had a bullet hole in it and parts of the guy's brains were spattered in it so I didn't think it would be in good taste to send it especially after knowing how things like that affect you. And another thing, I'd hate to lose an arm or a leg picking souvenirs up in Germany. Everything is booby trapped, even the dead. I think you'd rather have me come back in one piece even if you don't receive any souvenirs."

110

The last letter came months later. It distinguished itself from the rest because it had been mailed in a Red Cross envelope.

Dear Marge,
I know you've been very worried since you haven't heard anything from me in awhile. I am fine, but I've been in a German hospital and then in this place for three months. Here are the basic details. I was going on another of those trips of mine and I had a new driver with me. He was driving at the time. We slid on some ice and we hit a tree head-on. I broke my right leg (compound fracture) and got a few cuts around my face. My driver was knocked out. It took the Germans several days to get us to a hospital, and after this miserable cast was put on, they moved us to this place. It's called Stalag ___ (I'm sure the censors would blacken the name so I'm not going to bother to write it) I'm doing okay here. They have to treat us decently because of the Geneva Convention rules. I know you might be shocked by this, but believe me, dear, I am okay. Very soon this will be over, and I'll be stateside again."

What had happened to his father in that German prison? Phil had questioned his mother and he knew she was being honest when she said that he would never talk about it. "All I can tell you, Phil, is that when he came home, he was not the same strong, confident man I had married. He said he could not face a college classroom again, even though the GI Bill was available to him. He did odd jobs around town and the super in our apartment hired him to do some stuff too. We were struggling, even though I had a job as a receptionist in a doctor's office downtown."

Margaret Perrero had always treated her son like an adult. She was being honest with him now, he knew. "You were born three years after the war was over. For a few months, he seemed better. He got a job at the parts plant in Oneida. I thought everything was going to be okay, but then he would leave the house to go to work and disappear for days at a time. When he came home, he was in a disgusting state. He stank like he'd been sleeping in garbage cans and he would lie in bed, sick for days. Of course, he lost the job. The poor man was so miserable, Phil. When you turned two, he told me he had to go away, and to tell you the truth, by then, it was a relief."

"Where did he go?" he had asked his mother.

"The cards he sent those first couple of years had postmarks from places out west, Oregon, California, Nevada. He always asked how you were, but of course, I didn't know how I could answer him. There was never a return address."

His mother's advice always ended these conversations. "Don't blame your father, don't hate him for leaving. The war destroyed him. Try to put yourself in his shoes, Phil."

He rifles through the leather bag and pulls out a black and white photo of his father that his mother had taken. Phil, just a few months old, was in his arms. He stares at the picture of the handsome stranger. He is wearing a glaringly white tee-shirt. Thick, dark pompadour, combed back. Cigarette dangling from his lips; maybe that's why he holds his son so far away from his chest, like he is passing him to someone in the distance. His gaze is turned away from the baby; he stares directly into the camera lens.

Phil looks intently at the picture and into his father's eyes. An objective observer might see a vacancy in them, a paralysis of all emotion. But Phil can see through the ruse. As he thinks back to his mother's words, the irony strikes him with a force that is physical. He *is* walking in his father's shoes now, limping along and struggling every step of the way.

The sun shines off of the glossy black and white snapshot in his hands. Here is the answer he has come to Waikiki in search of, but it is not the one he wants.

Try as he might to alter them while he is awake, Phil knows he will continue to be haunted by his nightmares. Viet Nam and his time there have changed him for good. He will be running away from those memories for the rest of his life, his shame following close behind. He will be a prisoner of war, just as his father had been.

For the last time, Phil ties up the stack of letters and photos and puts them into the black leather bag.

Chapter Eight — Hearts and Minds

They are sitting in a circle, her favorite geometric pattern for the classroom. It is the perfect arrangement for the dynamism the teacher seeks. Often, she has several small groups reading, discussing, studying in smaller circles, but today, the whole class is arranged in one large sphere. It is populated by twenty students, an extremely diverse group in terms of age, income, and social class. It is as if they were hand picked and joined together to prove some sociologist's weird thesis. This assemblage is representative of the typical community college student spectrum, and Leigh Ann has always been challenged, in a positive way, by the crazy assortment of people who enroll in her classes.

The shiny blonde beauty sitting in the desk to her left is trying not to offend the professor, but she is obviously frustrated and so she speaks up. "Why do we have to read this? It's written in a foreign language," she says.

Leigh Ann smiles at her. She loves this kind of baiting from her students. Other educators might call it a teachable moment. Leigh Ann sees it as a catalyst and an opportunity to display her gift. As she stands up, the familiar burst of energy travels from her head to her feet. In a gesture her students witness daily in this class, the professor slides her glasses off her face and onto her head. They sit on top of her hair, like a tiara. She is a queen and she is presiding over her loyal subjects. She begins to walk the inside diameter of the circle.

"So... I want you, " she gently commands them as she walks, " to put yourself in this young guy's shoes. You're home from college, not on a regular break from school, but to bury a beloved parent, one whose death has come as a complete shock to you and everyone else in Denmark. Your friends, guys you've grown up with and trust, tell you they've spotted a ghost walking around the castle, your home. You are skeptical, but at midnight, he appears to *you*, and he looks an awfully lot like who he says he is: your dead father, who died weeks ago, reportedly from a snake bite. You are starting to believe that it's really him, the King, your father. And then he tells you, this is not exactly how it came down, this early demise of his. As a matter of fact, he tells you, it was your uncle, now married to your mother and wearing his dead brother's crown, who snuck up on him while he slept and poisoned him..."

One of the three boys she has mentally lumped together as The Jocks says, "This *does* sound like my life." There is some laughter, but it doesn't break the spell that Leigh Ann, in one of her favorite roles, has cast upon them. She continues her globular dance, and looks, one at a time, at their rapt faces. They are with the Young Prince. They are with *her*. *There's no place like home, there's no place like home*," Leigh Ann silently chants.

"And what does this ghost/father ask of his astonished son? " she questions, as she walks around the sphere, eyes locking into those of the spellbound listeners. The rapt expressions on their upturned faces remind her of the days when her children were small and she made up stories that had intrigued and delighted them.

"He says," she rises to her theatrical voice, and raps and beats out the iambic pentameter on a smiling student's desktop. ""Let not' the roy'al bed' of Den'mark be'/ A couch' for lux'ury' and damn'ed incest'.'" They love it. Leigh Ann loves it. Her students are satisfied customers.

"Damn! The dead King wants him to kill his uncle and mother, doesn't he?" one of her criminal justice majors says. He looks down at his book and quotes the ghost's line, "'Revenge this foul and most unnatural murder.' That's what he wants him to do, right?"

Weird Charlotte speaks up in her grating voice. Leigh Ann silently chastens herself for the secret nickname she has given the girl. But she can't help it. Lately, the kid has been more unkempt and smellier than ever before, as if she is making extra efforts to repel the people around her. And she has become the bane of Leigh Ann's existence outside of the classroom, too.

Nooo… she is close to shouting. "Not the mother! Only the uncle!" She picks the book up and brings it close to her thick lenses. "The Ghost says, 'However thou pursuest this act/ Taint not thy mind, nor let thy soul contrive/ Against thy mother aught/Leave her to heaven/And to those thorns that in her bosom lodge/ To prick and sting her.'" Her reading is painfully slow. Leigh Ann recognizes impatience on the faces of several students in the circle. She needs to reel them back into her arena.

"Love the way you scholars are going to the text of the play to back up your ideas!" she says.

Leigh Ann is a master at boosting the morale and building confidence in these Developmental Students. Developmental in this institution means, just-barely-made-it-out-of-high-school-after-five-or-six-years. She forbids the students to refer to the class as the Mentals, which at the beginning of the semester, someone always attempts to do. The course is a pre-requisite for students who did not achieve a certain score on the entrance test that indicates that they are ready to handle college level material. Leigh Ann's dean assigns her this class semester after semester, hoping these reticent students will finally wear her down, and that she will retire. And semester after semester, she brings out the best efforts of these people, because they feel safe and accepted in her classroom. And she does not retire.

Her graduate school mentor, Jim Courts, would be proud of her. He had come out of the early Ann Arbor movement, where the prototype for student-centered teaching was developed. In his method classes, Leigh Ann and her classmates had read, studied, and experimented with the ideas that came from the minds and books of progressive thinkers: Neil Postman's *Teaching As A Subversive Activity,* Janet Emig's *The Composition Process of Twelfth Graders,* Peter Elbow's *Writing Without Teachers.* Leigh Ann and all of Courts' young education revolutionaries were going to use literature and composition to teach students to be free-thinking citizens of a liberated world. They would follow the ideals of Thomas Jefferson. They were going to tear down the walls of the classroom and have no intrusive boundaries obstructing free thought.

All these years later, Leigh Ann has moved beyond even this reformist pedagogy to the level of radical artist. Her classroom is her theater, and student-centered as it may be, she is its starring performer. She is a skilled architect, and at the same time, a dinosaur who refuses to become extinct. This past semester, she had been offered an early retirement incentive, but once again, she refused it. What these paper pushers don't understand or appreciate is that it is not only her skill as a teacher, but her compassion as a person that fills her classes each semester.

She gets the most out of these individuals because she extends her empathy and understanding to them. In return, they want to do their best for her. Year after year, her student evaluations are glowing. She establishes relationships with many of them that last beyond the two years in which they work for an Associate's degree. Those who stay in the area, and that is the majority, become part of the community at large, and because of their rewarding experiences in Leigh Ann's classroom, they support the college as alumni. And so, although she will buck his authority, her dean knows that in the end, popular professors like her can fill the seats of a struggling institution.

      In this prescribed-core curriculum- humanities-snuffing- assessment-crazed period of education, which is marking her fourth decade of teaching, she flips the bird at the powers-who-be, and each day in her classroom she does it Her Way. *She* chooses the texts they will read. She never consults her English colleagues before designing a syllabus. She rarely lectures. She shapes her lessons so that they are experiential. When her students read the Odyssey, she challenges them to define and write about their own quests. When they study Antigone, she asks them to think and explore the corruption they see and struggle against in their own world. And when they write for her class, they trust her with the details of their sometimes sad and lonely existences, because she openly admits to them that the world makes her feel vulnerable, too.

"I've been abandoned by someone I loved," she says to them now. " He didn't have me killed, but there were days when I felt that he may as well have." She is walking slowly inside the circle, pausing in front of each of them. She is doing her teacher's striptease, peeling off the professor layers to expose the person beneath. They are spellbound.

"I wished back then that 'this too too solid flesh would melt,'" she sweeps her hand down the length of her body, but all eyes stay focused on her face. Silence. And then she says, "If it weren't for Lilly and David and my students, I might have…"

Leigh Ann is aware of her colleagues' opinions about her teaching techniques. Their judgments seem to be divided right along an age group fault line. Throughout the years and at the several colleges where she has taught, the younger faculty members aspire to be her; older teachers find her methods to be misguided and manipulative. These are the jealous peers, she feels, annoyed by the high enrollment she always has, while their own barren composition or lit classrooms look like an epidemic has swept the campus.

Leigh Ann is popular with the students, yes, but among them, she does not have a reputation for being "easy". Her standards are high. She works very hard. She knows her stuff, and she enforces the college's attendance policy, unlike many of her colleagues who worry about the drop-out rates in their classes and how that could impact their employment.

Now, she continues to move inside the circle at a slower pace. While she speaks about the tragedy in her own life, she pauses to look into the eyes of several of the twenty enthralled faces. Red baseball cap boy, elbow on desk, chin in hand, stares back. Young mother, criminal justice guy, middle-aged and unemployed man, black basketball player from New York City, all feel her pain in that moment. Charlotte's eyes through her thick lenses look damp and bloodshot. She has been excitedly nodding throughout Leigh Ann's soliloquy.

The teacher moves to the middle of the circle, and very slowly spins, the needle in the compass. "So why should we read *Hamlet*?" she asks. They want the answer. They wait for it, even though the class is officially over. Other students spill out from other classrooms, but Leigh Ann's audience waits.

And then she says, "*You* tell *me*."

She makes the assignment and the class is over. A few students stay behind to get some clarification about the essay she wants. A couple are obviously lingering because they enjoy being in her presence. And then, everyone but Charlotte is gone.

"I know how you felt, when your husband left you," the girl says now. She is biting what is left of her fingernails. She stops and picks up a picture of Lilly and David from Leigh Ann's desk. A rare smile flits across her face as she sets it back down. The teacher feels a shiver prickle the back of her neck.

Leigh Ann knows that her charisma in the classroom can sometimes attract the neediest of kids. Typically, this type of student might take every class she teaches within the two-year span of their community college endeavor. They drop by during her office hours, just to 'hang' and to soak up more of the teacher's attention. Sometimes they invite her out for a beer after class. A few have called her crying late at night.

A long time ago, when she was still at Vassar, one actually fell in "love" with her. He started following her in his car when she left the campus. There were many hang-up calls back in that day before cell phones. Peter had had to call the police when flowers were delivered to the house with a card that professed the student's love and his belief that if she had his baby, it would be the Christ child risen again. After the police warned him to stay away from her, she never saw him again.

And now Charlotte is her problem. Harmless, unlike her stalker from years ago, but a pest nevertheless. From the first day of the first class in which she was enrolled, she has felt perfectly justified in calling and texting the professor. Now that Leigh Ann lives alone, the midnight and beyond messages are becoming more than bothersome. Sometimes, she is awakened from a deep sleep by the ding of her phone, and she panics, thinking Lilly or David has been in an accident.

Charlotte sets the picture frame back on her desk and says, "He didn't deserve you."

Leigh Ann gives her a brief smile. She never wants to patronize her students, but, really, how can a twenty-something know what it feels like to have your partner of twenty-five years leave you? Yes, they had been unhappy for a long time, but Leigh Ann had a pit bull's tenacity when it came to holding on to a commitment. It had been six years since she woke up alone and found the post-it note on the kitchen table; she fought it tooth and nail for the first four years, even though her kids wished she would get it over with and move on. But now, her divorce is final.

She will turn fifty-nine in April. She has lost weight since her husband left, and she has lately been using her faculty privilege- a free membership at the Y; last week one of her male students told her that she looks "ripped". She even had a little laser treatment on her face recently to get rid of some of the imperfections and wrinkles. Yes, she does look good, and although Peter's abandonment of her and their marriage has left an indelible scar, the independence she did not ask for this late in life is an unexpected benefit.

And lately, she is feeling good enough to consider what it would be like to have someone in her life again. So far, there has not been even a single flirtation, never mind a date, in all these years. She had made up her mind that she would never be loved again, and her friends tell her that the reason she hasn't met anyone is that she is sending out that vibe to potential suitors.

That is why the emails she has recently exchanged with a college boyfriend have been, well, she has to admit it, *thrilling.* A man from her past who has actually been thinking about her after decades, one who shared Fredonia and the 60's with her, and one who has taken the time to search for her! Mind blowing and flattering.

Standing in front of her is this pathetic, overweight, country kid, who has probably never been as far away as Buffalo, and who, as she admits in much of her writing, has never had a boyfriend; yet she thinks she understands Leigh Ann's pain. She keeps it simple, so as not to engage her any longer. "Thanks, Charlotte." She gathers up her things, puts them in her briefcase, and walks with the girl to the classroom door.

"Can I call you later, if I need help with the assignment?" Well, this is an improvement. She usually doesn't ask. Last week, as Leigh Ann pulled into her driveway, she saw a piece of blue paper taped to her front door. She felt a little sick to her stomach as she read it: *Please call me. Charlotte.* Once inside she had ripped the note into tiny pieces.

"If you get totally stuck, sure," she says over her shoulder and heads to the faculty parking lot. As she answers her, Leigh Ann has a rare flash of déjà vu. She had said those same words to the girl last semester, when a blizzard had hit the county and closed the campus. That morning, Leigh Ann had decided to drive the half-mile from her home to the vacated college to work in her office. She was sitting at her desk listening to the Beatles' White Album and looking at her computer screen when she heard wet, squeaking footsteps coming down the abandoned English suite hallway.

Standing in the doorway was Charlotte, her height and weight accentuated by a one-size-too-small Carhartt parka. Her glasses had steamed up in reaction to the building's overheated environment. Leigh Ann could not suppress a startled little jump. "Charlotte, what are you doing here? Don't you know that the campus is closed. There are no classes today."

"My brother had early basketball practice this morning, so he brought me in at 6:30, before the place shut, I guess. I've been calling his cell, but he's not picking up. Can I hang out in here for awhile?" she asked.

"Sure." Trying not to sound resentful for the girl's intrusion on her quiet workspace she added, "Would you like some coffee?"

Charlotte looked at her as if she had been offered much more than caffeine. "That would be great." The girl smiled, and Leigh Ann involuntarily shuddered. She was creeped out by this kid and it pissed her off. Trying hard to fight off her revulsion, the teacher headed to the faculty lounge to make coffee for the two of them. As she set the cups and the vending machine snacks on a small tray, she resolved to extend herself to this poor girl. Charlotte had written about her life in several compositions this semester, and it is bleak, to say the least. Leigh Ann squared her shoulders and walked back into the suite of English offices.

As she concentrated on not slopping the coffee over the sides of the mugs, she heard her office printer working. It can't be, she thought. When she walked in, Charlotte was sitting in the professor's chair, looking at her computer monitor.

"What are you doing?" Be nice, Leigh Ann. Be nice, she had warned herself.

Charlotte startled. "Oh, sorry. My phone has one bar left, so I got online to check the road and school closings. I also printed the numbers for the high school offices, so I can call them later to try to reach my brother. Was that okay?" She looked pathetic.

"Sure, but I wish you had asked first." Damn, why was it so hard not to feel like a bitch around this girl? She set the tray down, and as they drank their coffee, the courtyard vista outside Leigh Ann's office window disappeared, obliterated by the blowing white.

"Do you have any friends or relatives here in the city?" she asked, dreading the answer.

"No. There's no one. Do you think I could stay at your house until I can get a hold of my brother?" The timid tone seemed unnatural to the girl, whose voice typically agitated anyone within earshot.

Damn it! Here it was again, that Charlotte ambivalence: she felt sorry for the kid, and at the same time she was anxious to be out from under the dark shadow that she cast. "Sure, if you're really stuck," Leigh Ann heard herself say.

Late in the afternoon, she did get a hold of her brother, who told her that for the last hour he had been trying to charge the battery of his pick-up, but it was dead. Their father was nowhere to be found. Leigh Ann looked outside at the blowing snow. She really didn't want to have the girl stay overnight in her home, but more than that, she did not want to drive out into the boonies in this storm.

Charlotte's sleepover was not the nightmare Leigh Ann had anticipated. Apart from her picking up and asking about every object in the study, and looking at every picture on every wall on the first floor, the girl was less annoying than she was in the classroom. Leigh Ann made a quick sauce with the vegetables she had roasted over the weekend and tossed a salad. She stopped in front of the wine rack. No, it wouldn't do to get a buzz on with this weirdo in the house. Oops, there she went again. Random, nasty thoughts about another human being. One who declared the pasta and tossed salad was her first gourmet meal ever. Guilt washed over her for the tenth time that day.

But when it came time to think about sleeping arrangements, Leigh Ann did not feel culpable enough to let the girl sleep in one of the two bedrooms across from her own on the second floor. Handing her sheets, a blanket, and a pillow, she pointed Charlotte in the direction of the pull out in the study and told her to make herself at home. The television would be all hers for the rest of the night. Leigh Ann headed upstairs to her bedroom and locked the door behind her.

In the morning, which for Leigh Ann, noon on a Saturday still counted as morning, Charlotte was gone. The sheets and blanket were neatly folded, the bed had been converted back into a couch. There was a note on the kitchen table.

Thank you for everything. I had a blast!
Charlotte.

Leigh Ann let out an involuntary sigh of relief. She realized she was breathing deeply for the first time since Charlotte had walked into her office yesterday. It had all worked out, though. She had helped a student in need, and it was all fine. She silently promised to do her level best to be tolerant and kind to this kid from now on. She had had no idea that snowy morning how impossible it would become to uphold this pledge.

After the storm, Charlotte called, emailed, and/or texted her everyday. Some days she would do all three. By the second semester, when she enrolled in her Developmental Writing About Literature class, Leigh Ann had changed her mind about extending kindheartedness to the girl. Her incessant efforts to reach her had practically ruined her winter break with her kids in California.

"Tell the dean. Change your number. Tell the bitch to stop," Lilly and David, always exasperated by their mother's passivity, told her.

No, she would handle this mess her way. By ignoring the girl's attempts to reach out to her. Leigh Ann's marriage had provided her with years of practice with this strategy.

Now, on this day one month away from the end of the semester, she walks away from the girl and her neediness. Leigh Ann gets into her car and backs out. As she pulls into the exit lane to head off campus, she glances at her rearview mirror. Charlotte is standing in Leigh Ann's empty parking space, waving.

"Whew," she says out loud, like a woman who has dodged a bullet. The teaching week is behind her, and so is this creepy kid. Leigh Ann happily turns up the radio. On this sunny Friday in late April, she is beginning to feel great. She is headed out for a drink with some colleagues at Chimera's, a place where the few professionals in this small city go for Happy Hour.

By five o'clock, she is laughing at something her friend Adam has said. She never would have believed that she could feel this carefree again after the shock of Peter leaving.

She is at the bar ordering another Pinot Noir, when her cell phone rings. She checks the ID to make sure it is not one of her kids and then Leigh Ann will do what she always does when she sees Charlotte's number come up on her phone screen. She will hit End Call and off this pest will scurry to her voice mail. There are already dozens of calls from her this week alone on her log. Leigh Ann has not listened to one.

"Hey, Leigh, have you got a hot lover stashed away somewhere?" Adam asks, before she can mute the notification whistle on her phone.

"No, just a pain-in-the-ass student," she says in a tone that implies that everyone has one of these. Three other colleagues join them at the bar in time to hear her reply.

"Texting you?" Leslie, a sociology professor practically shouts. She is obviously incredulous and maybe a little buzzed. "About?"

"Nothing. She's a Seinfeld-texter. She sends messages that are about nothing," Leigh Ann responds. A few uncomfortable chuckles follow her attempt to make a joke.

"How did a student get your cell number?" Dale, a member of her department asks. She ignores his question. It's none of his business anyway.

"Have you told the dean? Or the kid's counselor?" Her friend Adam Messinger is a therapist who works at the college counseling center part time, so he has a professional interest and reason for asking the question.

Leigh Ann shrugs and sips her wine. Then she shakes her head in response to Adam. Charlotte's texts are easy enough to ignore. They are typically brief, banal, and adolescent. *My dad grounded my brother; now i have no ride tonight, U hear about the fire at my neighbor's? Do u think I should major in nursing or criminal justice? Liked the sweater u wore Wed.*

She notices that a few of her friends have backed away from the bar and are standing in smaller clusters with their wine glasses and beer bottles. Eyes are glancing her way, and it is obvious they are discussing her and the texting scandal. She's used to this kind of skepticism about her relationship with her students. Peter had nagged her through the years about her inability to establish professional boundaries. Well, he is out of her life now, and she refuses to permit her ex-husband's scorn or her colleagues' gossip to ruin her night.

Leigh Ann wishes everyone a good weekend and leaves the bar. At home in her kitchen, she heats up last night's leftovers and has one more glass of wine. She puts on her most comfortable sweats, and settles down in front of the television. But her phone's buzzing vibration distracts her throughout the movie she is trying to watch. When the film is over, irritated, she turns off the TV and her phone and heads upstairs to her bed.

On Saturday morning, just before she leaves to do some grocery shopping, she turns her cell phone on. She scrolls through dozens of texts, all from Charlotte. The first one had been sent at 1:45 in the morning, and she reads it all the way through. *Mark me. My hour is almost come when I to sulph'rous and tormenting flames must render up myself.* Somewhere in the middle of the thirty-some messages she reads, *O wicked wits and gifts that have the power so to seduce won to his shameful lust The will of my most seeming virtuous queen.* And she reads the last one: *Adieu, adieu, adieu! Remember me!*

There are ten voice mails, too. She erases each one without listening to them. Jesus, this girl is annoying. She is stealing some of Leigh Ann's precious time outside of the classroom and she is feeling righteously pissed. Up until now she had been gentle with the girl. She had done her best to ignore her. But on Monday, she'll ask her to meet her in her office and she will tell her in no uncertain terms that she is to stop calling and texting her.

Her thoughts are interrupted by an engine turning over in her driveway. She looks out just in time to see a rusty, red pick-up backing out. Charlotte, who as far as she knows, does not have a license, is behind the wheel. Yes, she will certainly have that talk with her on Monday.

The rest of her weekend is Charlotte-free. Leigh Ann goes to a Blues Fest in Ellicottville with some old friends. Sunday she has enough of a hangover that she easily convinces herself that she can grade those Hamlet essays tomorrow in her campus office. Today will be spent answering emails, writing her next column for *The Ellicottville Courier*, and catching up on the three *Breaking Bad* episodes on her DVR.

Monday morning she feels rested. Because she hates conflict more than anything, she dreads seeing Charlotte, but she is resolved. The situation is out of control and she needs to deal with it. When she enters her classroom she is surprised to discover no Charlotte, who is often late, but never absent. Good. Maybe she is embarrassed and has come to the conclusion herself that Leigh Ann does not deserve these inappropriate intrusions.

After class, she heads to her office and turns on her computer. Scrolling through her email, she is pleased to see that all twenty Developmental students have posted their *Hamlet* essays. She squares her shoulders and begins to read.

Two hours later, Leigh Ann picks up the phone and dials. "Please let me speak to whichever counselor is assigned to Charlotte White. It's an emergency!"

Chapter Nine — To Be

Charlotte White   Writing About Literature
April 3, 2009   Professor LA Fray

Task: Literary critics throughout the centuries since Shakespeare wrote his most famous play have noted that the character of Hamlet possesses universal qualities, and that his struggles, in one way or another, represent those of all of us. What personal discoveries have you made by reading the play? Be sure to underscore your ideas by referring to lines from the text.

I see myself in the play Hamlet. I have struggled a lot in my life. I have been alone. I pretty much have no friends, even when I was a child. My mom has been gone since I was 9. I have been in charge of my brothers and sisters since then. My dad has no interest in us. He is an alcoholic. He has sleazy girlfriends.

Like Hamlet I was depressed and struggled with what I should do. Then one night a couple of years ago while I lay in bed I was not visited by a ghost but by a Voice. The Voice seemed to know everything about me and my life. Right before I fell asleep, it would come to me and guide me. It would tell me I was okay that I should ignore all of the people who hated me or that Bridget one of my dad's girlfriends was going to die soon so I didn't need to worry about her insults and slaps.

One night when things were really bad in my life the Voice came to me and gave me instructions on how to end everything. We made a plan that I would shoot myself in the barn. But just like Hamlet I started to have doubts about the Voice, like he did about his father's ghost. ("The spirit that I have seen/May be a devil; and the devil hath power/ T' assume a pleasing shape.")

People have always called me crazy. Maybe I was and there was no Voice. ("And perhaps out of my weakness and my melancholy,/ As he is very potent with such spirits,/ Abuses to damn me.") And then I started college and the Voice left me for awhile.

When it came back to me it was more powerful than ever. I have never been a strong person. Before the Voice came like Hamlet I had a hard time making up my mind. ("To be, or not to be; that is the question.") But when the Voice came back to me I started to feel like all of my decisions were right.

The Voice sees what others cannot. It knows what is best for me. Professor Fray since I first met you the Voice has told me that you are good. Not just that you are a good teacher and person but that you are good for me. That I need to be near you always so that my life does not fall apart again. That is why I have to talk to you or try anyway every day. The Voice tells me that you don't know how good you are. It tells me that people always want to destroy what's good and that you are in constant danger of this happening. Something or Someone wants to take you away from me and this world. The Voice tells me it is my job to stay close to you and take care of you. That is my heroic quest like we have read and talked about this semester. Like Hamlet protecting Gertrude from Claudius

I have to protect you. I have to take action.

Charlotte rereads her essay. She is satisfied. She hits Submit. Then she pulls out the sheet of paper with all of the passwords that she had found on Leigh Ann's desk the night of the blizzard. She runs her finger down the list and pauses on the one she has been looking for. With a satisfied smile, Charlotte logs onto the teacher's personal email account.

Chapter Ten — Mission

The atomic clock projects a gigantic 3:00 onto the ceiling. Phil is once again summoned by it, and his wife's quiet breathing over the past hour reassures him that all systems are go; he will not be kept from his task, as he had been last night when Rosie had awakened and asked if he had had a nightmare. He plants his bare feet on the floor and stands still for a moment. Then he tiptoes out of their bedroom and steals down the creaky thirteen stairs to his den.

Without a discernible sound, he closes the door and turns on his laptop. Or is it his time machine? This whacky thought causes him to snort out loud. Oh, Jesus. Don't wake up Rosie, asshole, he silently chastises himself. What has happened to his cool, calm self? Lately, he cannot seem to control his reactions.

Remarkably, this past month he has been experiencing a full range of feelings and emotions. Curiosity, anticipation, hope, happiness, a spectrum of sensations that has transferred to his pulse, his sweat glands, his circulatory system, his facial muscles. Since the hell of the Mekong Delta, except for his life-long passion for fast cars and motorcycles, he strives for a mindset of indifference. After all these years of idling in neutral, lately Phil feels like he is at the mercy of these motley emotions.

Decades before, he had designed for himself a protective disguise of dispassion. He can trace its inception back to the day he landed at La Guardia, back on American soil for the first time in four years. Phil had not considered Hawaii, where he was based after Vietnam, an authentic part of his homeland... too many jungle plants and brown people. In those ways, it was very much like Nam and nothing at all like the northeastern United States. Besides, for the first six months after his tour in Vietnam, he had been so fucked up, he might as well have been on Mars.

There was no one at the arrival gate that day to greet Phil, not that he had expected that there would be. He was going to catch the Amtrak from Penn Station back home to Utica. He did not want his mother to have to take the day off from work, and besides her, there was no one else from his hometown that he would have wanted to see.

He continued walking, following the signs directing travelers to the baggage claim area. This concourse went on for miles, he thought to himself. He took long strides, trying to get the blood flowing after his trans-oceanic trip. As he did, he was aware that to a casual observer, he might appear to be a young man in the prime of his life. His uniform with its three medals flashing on his chest distinguished him from most of the commuters that morning, although he had seen some Marines on his flight.

He turned left, following the sign for the escalator. It was the quickest way to get to the ground floor of the terminal where he would pick up his duffel bag. He stepped onto it, and from somewhere behind him came a muffled male voice, but the disgust in the tone was not muted at all. "Fucking baby killer." Phil fixed his eyes in front of him, concentrating on a buzzing sound that seemed to come from the conveyer belt of the escalator. He stretched his long legs forward, and skipping a couple of steps, planted his feet on the floor and continued walking toward his destination.

Passing him in the opposite direction, a woman who appeared to be around his mother's age looked directly at him and, narrowing her eyes, hissed,

"Barbarian!" He felt her hatred like a bullet, but his face registered nothing.

When he reached the baggage claim area, a man not much younger than Phil, long-haired and wearing an Army jacket, stood in the claim line next to him. He was looking Phil up and down, staring rudely at his uniform. He opened his mouth and asked a rhetorical, "How does it feel to be a Fascist pig?" Phil gazed blankly back into the kid's eyes.

He had landed only thirty minutes before, and already he had been exposed. These strangers had recognized his shame. So on this day Phil began to put into practice the deceit that would make it possible for him to function in his post-war world. He vowed that after today, he would not willingly be a target for the scorn of others. He would take off the uniform forever, and put on in its place an attitude and demeanor that was devoid of emotion. And so he did, and after a very short time, his detachment became genuine.

By the time of his mother's wake months later, he had perfected this indifference, so much so, that as he stood at her coffin looking down at her, he could not feel sadness.

He had loved his mother. He had always admired her for her courage especially, although he had never told her that. As a young girl, she had immigrated alone to a strange new country. She had lived for the first year with a cousin in Brooklyn until she got a job and moved by herself to Albany. Young Margaret Andolina possessed a fierce determination not only to assimilate, but to prosper in her new homeland. The United States offered a rich bounty of opportunities for anyone who was not afraid of hard work, she had told Phil from the time he was in elementary school. He was *so lucky* to have been born here, she said again and again. It wasn't a perfect place, America, but it was the best place on earth to live, she told her son.

Margaret had struggled, through the Depression, like most people of her generation. When the Second World War broke out, she suffered, knowing that her own family members still living in Italy were enemies of the United States. And then she lost her husband to that war. After his imprisonment in the Stalag, he could not bear to share his pain with his family, so he had left her alone to raise their son. She was a single parent in a small city in America before the time that this status was considered commonplace. From the time he was a toddler, Phil and his mother were viewed as an anomaly, an aberration that was often viewed as suspicious by the members of normal, nuclear families. But the regard of others had never been a priority for Margaret Perrero. Once Frank was gone, she worked full-time and took care of her son the rest of the time; these were her main concerns in life.

College had always been her dream for him, and so she was a firm guardian of his good grades in high school. When he was accepted at Fredonia, she made a four-year plan so that he would not have to take out any loans. Margaret paid the half of his tuition his work-study job did not cover, and she managed every two weeks to send him some "pizza and beer money" too.

She had been disappointed when he dropped out and very upset that he had enlisted, but her love and dedication to him were unwavering. She who had known him best had known nothing about what his life had become once he had joined the army. Her ignorance, of course, was not her fault. Phil knew all of these things about his mother, but what he felt as he looked at her for the last time in her casket was a cool estrangement.

After his mother's death, Phil carried this sense of detached alienation with him. Even as he made efforts to return to the life he had left before his years in the service, his disconnection prevailed. He tried to go back to college to finish his history degree at Herkimer Community, but from the first day he walked into a classroom, he could not engage with or take seriously anything the professors were saying. He had been such a passionate sponge of a student before the war, he thought, disgusted by the memory of his naive younger self. Now, reading his American history textbooks and listening to class discussions about government and foreign policy sickened him. He knew better, or worse, actually, than these corporately manufactured stories of his country. He had witnessed first-hand what the United States government did in the guise of spreading democracy.

The teens who were his classmates cast sidelong glances at him from time to time. It seemed that they could smell the Alien on him. He felt so much bigger than them, although he was only a few years older. His body mass seemed to overfill the desks, the classrooms. And at the same time, he felt shrunken inside. The other students looked so innocent, so stupid to him. They didn't know shit or they could not have been so incredibly joyful. Hypnotically running through his head during much of what would be his final semester of college was the Leon Russell lyric, " He's a stranger in a strange land."

When Phil dropped out of college for the second time, he enrolled in a job-training program at the local BOCES center, paid for by the army. He had chosen to learn how to become a glazier by default. It was the only course left that had not been filled by the dozens of other returning, unemployed veterans.

He found the training surprisingly satisfying. He enjoyed learning about the different types of glass, and he studied the structural supports used in various types of architecture. He was good at the hands-on stuff too. He liked the feel of the tools, the cold steel in his hands. The measuring and cutting, the focus he needed to accurately fit the glass into the small panels, and at the same time avoid slashing himself, provided him with a satisfying sense of completeness. This education was a finite endeavor. All of it made sense. There was no theoretical bullshit or lies like those he had encountered in the army or in his college courses.

His instructors noticed him. He was more serious and mature than the other guys in the program, and they suggested he apply for an apprenticeship with a local glazier contracting company. Why not, he thought. He had no other options.

The day that Phil walked into the office of Pettit Glass, the receptionist greeted him with a polite smile followed by a bright glimmer of recognition. "You're Phil Perrero, right?" she asked. She looked vaguely familiar, and then he recognized her. Rose Pettit from high school. They had laughed and carried on throughout their 10th grade English class. She was still pretty. And still friendly.

This was her father's company. Years later she told him that her old man had not wanted him for the apprenticeship spot, but Rose had persuaded him. And Phil had learned so quickly and had been so meticulous on the job sites, her father hired him without her having to pressure him at all. Within five years, he was foreman on all of the firm's specialty jobs. He was the guy who would fearlessly climb ten stories on the scaffolding to replace windows in the state capitol building in Albany. Whenever the firm was hired to do replacement stained glass work in homes and cathedrals in the tri-state area, Phil Perrero was the glazier who did this demanding and intricate work. When their first daughter was born, Rose's father took Phil off the scaffold. After the old man had died and the new owner took over, Phil became the company's commercial consultant, the position he had held for the last thirty years.

He had married Rose the year he was hired as a full-time employee. He hadn't known that she had had a huge crush on him in high school. He was so funny, and so sure of himself as a seventeen-year-old. But then he had gone away to college, and they lost touch. She was surprised to hear through the grapevine that he had dropped out of Fredonia and joined the army. When she saw him that day at the office, it was for the first time in several years. He had changed. The youthful intensity she remembered was gone, replaced by a low key, mature coolness. She had asked him to go for a drink that night, and six months later, they were married.

Within a few weeks of the honeymoon, Phil had his first nightmare. Rose was shocked by the terrible power it had over him. "Nam," he answered vaguely when she asked him what the dream was about. "Cowards," he said, but he never told her the details of that dream or the dozens of others that followed, but she could see that her husband was haunted by something horrific. She honored his wish not to talk about the war, but she could not stand to see him suffer. She made an appointment for him with a therapist at the VA. And she tolerated the pot smoking that took place whenever he was not working or sleeping. He stayed high throughout the weekends of the first two decades of their marriage, and although Rose knew his use was excessive, she mainly kept that opinion to herself. He seemed to be able to sleep through the night after smoking, and that was enough for her.

By the time he was in his fifties, the nightmares still afflicted him and the pot smoking was getting him nowhere. So he finally quit that habit. He had stopped going to therapy years before. He had told his wife it was total bullshit.

He and Rose were empty-nesters when he received the skin cancer diagnosis. The surgery had been successful. Phil just had to be examined at three-month intervals for the rest of his life. In spite of this positive outcome, Rose watched her husband become more and more withdrawn. What he had not told Rosie was that he had been to the specialist again, and the results of the biopsy were not good. All she knew was what she observed. He would sit alone in the dark of his study for hours at a time. She was afraid he would start drinking again, now that he had quit smoking weed. Three decades after she had called the first time, she reached out to the counseling center at the VA and set up an appointment for him, which he had kept.

"Phil, what makes you happy?"

He sat in front of the new shrink and thought about how much she reminded him of his youngest daughter. She was probably around her age. She had asked if she could call him by his first name, but for some reason, it was off-putting to have her address him with such familiarity. He tried to shake off the negativity. He would be honest with her. "Nothing," he said.

"So this lack of emotion, this 'zombie' state, as you've described it, would you say that you've felt that way since your surgery?"

"Way before that," he said. How was this kid going to help him? But he had no other options; he would let her lead him down any path she thought would help him get through this final chapter of his life. He told himself that this was the last therapist he would ever see, no matter what Rosie said. If she could not help him, he was done.

"You know there are very effective medications that can help with depression, Phil."

And there it was. A shrink's answer to everything. "I'm an addict and an alcoholic," he told her. "I came here to try to get some answers that don't involve altering my brain chemistry. I'd like to stay clear of substances."

"I understand," she said. He seriously doubted that.

"When was the last time you felt joy, Phil?" she asked him. A long silence filled the little sitting room that was her office. He was battling the urge to get up and walk out.

"I'd like you to spend some time before our next session thinking about my question. A lot of my clients find writing in a journal helps when they are looking back and reflecting on their past."

"Okay," he said. "And then what? After I unlock the memory of a happy time, I'll be able to feel something again?" He was trying his best not to sound like a sarcastic prick, but he wasn't sure he was succeeding.

"Not exactly. When you find the answer, you and I will work on getting back to that time, perhaps rediscovering that place again, in a spiritual sense, of course. Let's get together again in a couple of weeks and see what you've uncovered. In the meantime, keep up the running and weight lifting. Exercise is good for you."

Phil never sees the young therapist again. He does not keep a journal. He does not sit and meditate upon his past, but shortly after that first and last session with her, he has the answer to her question. He is shocked by the unexpected clarity he now has. Fate and coincidence have intervened. He has rediscovered that time and place, totally by chance.

Over the past few weeks since that discovery, he has been on an adventure. Phil believes that he has found the pathway to recover that "joy", but it is by a very unorthodox route. He has been traveling forward and backward simultaneously to reach it. Tonight, his pulse is racing; he can feel his heart pounding as he turns on his laptop. He has become the architect of something larger and more meaningful, at last.

Pure luck had given him the answer, but what Phil did with this knowledge would be much more complicated. His active undertaking of this mission had started the very night after he had had this revelation. It was just happenstance that he had gone on that road trip with Art that day. Just by chance, he had been guided back to that porch in Sidney. This time, he must get what he had come for. He sat down at his computer and searched for her on People Finder. He entered her last name + SUNY Fredonia + 1968. Her picture appeared on the screen in front of him within seconds. Her hair had darkened and had been tamed, but her eyes still radiated the same blue as her father's.

She was a college professor of English in a place about 250 miles away. Amazing! When they had hitchhiked to that Hendrix concert in Syracuse, she had been on academic probation. The directory listed awards she had received along with her published works. She currently wrote a weekly newspaper column called "*Convergences*" for *The Ellicottville Courier*. He took the title as a good omen. There was a link to a *Buffalo News* article covering her 2005 Chancellor's Excellence in Teaching Award. He had read it and discovered a town, a husband, grown children. He went back to the college directory where he found an office phone number, and an email address.

He had felt electrified by the results of his search, which was the only way he could have described it. He had a goofy visual from the old Boris Karloff version of Frankenstein. He was the dead monster, hooked up on that table. And this undertaking, the possibility that he could rediscover what had been his destiny was jump-starting him. Once he had found what looked like the path back to his happiness, he could not turn back.

The next night he had waited for Rose to fall asleep. He had crept down the stairs into the darkened study and written to Leigh Ann for the first time in forty years.

Hello,
I'm looking for a long lost friend of mine who had your name, in 1968 anyway. She was from Sidney, NY, and she attended Fredonia State in 1968 and I haven't seen her since then. I was hoping to re-connect with Leigh Ann.
If you aren't the Leigh Ann Fray I knew, please accept my apologies for inconveniencing you in any way. The fact that you were a Fredonia State student who graduated in 1972 seems to me to be a very unlikely coincidence. But, I understand that such flukes do happen and, again, offer apologies if I have bothered you.
Sincerely,
Phil Perrero

He hit send, turned off the computer, and went back to his bed. He tried not to toss and turn throughout the rest of that short night, but he had woken Rosie in spite of his best efforts.

At work the next morning, adrenaline overrode his grogginess when he scrolled through his email and read the subject line. **Re: Looking**. He clicked on the message and read.

Phil,
I am the Leigh Ann Fray you knew and with whom you saw Hendrix live!!! I am not in Sidney anymore, but I am back living and teaching in Western New York. How lovely to hear from you after all these years.
Leigh Ann

It was truly Leigh Ann; the Hendrix reference was proof positive! And not only had she responded quickly, but she had not told him to go to hell. He thought for a while about what he wanted to say to her, now that he had found her. He spent the better part of the morning composing his next message to her.

Hi Leigh Ann,
I felt sure it was you I had found, but I was afraid that you might not remember me or worse yet get upset that I tried to contact you after all these years. Here's why I started looking for you and how I found you. A couple of weeks ago a buddy of mine asked me if I wanted to ride my motorcycle up route 17 from Utica to Malone, NY with him. When he got off

the expressway for lunch in Sidney, I couldn't help
think of you, nothing romantic (I'm married), just
wondered how you were and how your life had gone.
We actually drove by your old house. So, when I got
home I did a Google search for you. I saw a couple of
pictures of you but wasn't sure until I saw a color
picture and recognized your blue eyes. It would be
nice to meet and talk about how our lives have gone.
It's been a long time and I have thought about you off
and on over the years and have wondered what if.
Please believe me that your memory is special to me
but it is just a memory of the past. I mean no harm or
offense.
-Phil

After he had written it, he had gone to Albany
on a job that had taken him out of the office for the rest
of the day, so his first chance to check for a response
from her was when he got back home. He turned on his
laptop, and there was her name and the Subject
"**GLAD**." As he read and reread her email, he realized
he had been waiting for this since as far back as 1969.

Phil,
I am so glad to hear from you. You hold a special
place in my memories as well, and I would very
much like to get together to talk, catch up, perhaps
be friends.
After twenty-five years of marriage, I am recently
divorced. I have two grown children who both are
musicians living on the west coast. Check my Face
Book page to see pictures of them and their bands.

Where are you living these days? I would enjoy
hearing from you again. My college years at
Fredonia were truly wonderful times, and certainly
you were a part of that. Let me hear from you.
Fondly,
Leigh Ann

His pulse was racing as he reread her words.

The sounds from the kitchen of Rosie preparing dinner

did not interfere with this part of his mission. He had

carefully planned and edited his first two emails, but he

composed this third message to her as he typed.

Dear Leigh Ann,
I was very sad to hear that you are divorced after
such a long marriage. Very sad. It must be hard
having your children so far away.
I've wanted to talk to you for a long time about a lot
of things. I have not been ready to do that, I guess,
until lately. It is by total accident that I found you
again, but I did, and know I think we should see each
other in person and talk.
Believe me, I'm not sure either of us can take the
conversation we might have. I would want you to be
prepared to have this conversation, too. It would be
a hard time for me and I think you too.
I don't want to cause you any pain by talking but I
would like to understand
what happened those many years ago. I realize now
that I acted like a little boy, even though I was 20 at
the time. But Leigh Ann, when I want to feel better
about everything, I just try to remember a special
night in the Union at Gregory Hall and what a pretty
young girl told me there.

I'm about 250 miles east of you. The weather is getting better and it will not be a hard ride. I'd like an invitation to visit you in Allegany, but even if you say come, I may decide not to. I'll probably come if you want me to. But please be certain you'll be okay.

Fondly,
Phil

He hit send.

The next two days were hell. There had been no answer to his last message.

So on this night, nervous and excited, once again he scans each address in his Inbox. The one he wants to see is still not there. Okay, a minor setback. He would have preferred an invitation from her, but after days of waiting for her reply, he decides he had at least given her a warning. His wife is leaving Friday to visit their daughter for a couple of days. The weather is supposed to be beautiful. It has to be now or never.

On Saturday morning he packs his saddlebags with a couple of changes of clothes, his rain gear, and the gift he has made for Leigh Ann. He had wound several sheets of bubble wrap around it so that it would survive the trip. He takes a long look at the home he and Rose have built together. Then he straddles his BMW, starts the engine, and begins his journey.

The bike runs smoothly as he heads downstate. He wonders what she will make of his close-cropped white hair, the wrinkles around his eyes. He is proud of his body. He has taken good care of it, as much as anyone his age can. And because he has, the doctor has said he may be able to beat this cancer thing. Yes, his body was alright. It was his head that had been the problem. No therapist could have talked him out of this burden of incompleteness he had carried with him all these years. Now he is in pursuit of the answer to the question: why had he lost her? As his speedometer hits 80, he feels as though he is on a pilgrimage that will cure him at last.

He gets off Route 86 at the first city exit. He spots the Marriot where he has optimistically reserved a room for the night. Pulling into the Kwik Fill across from the hotel, he pulls up to the pumps and turns off the ignition. He takes off his helmet and sunglasses and walks inside to pay for his gas. The fat girl at the counter looks pissed off, or maybe she appears that way to Phil because he is feeling almost giddy with excitement. He hands her his credit card. "Fifteen, please. Regular, on pump five." He goes to the back of the store and grabs a bottle of water from the cooler. As he walks back to the counter, he is certain the grumpy cashier is giving him the stink eye for some reason. He knows the card is good, so what's her problem?

He is surprised when she turns on the small town charm. "Nice bike!" Her voice is startlingly loud as she points to the BMW. "You on your way to someplace special?" Now she is wearing a strained smile.

"Nope. Visiting an old friend here in town." He returns her smile.

She hands him his card and the receipt, never taking her eyes off of him as he signs. As he opens the door, she shouts at his back, "Have a nice day, Mr. Perrero!"

"Yeah, you too," he says over his shoulder. He pumps the gas, puts on his glasses, helmet, and gloves and drives across the street to the hotel. As he gets off the bike and opens his saddlebag, he does a double take. Across the two-lane road, Phil can see that the fat clerk is looking out the front window of the convenience store. She seems to be staring at him. "Weirdo," he whispers to himself.

Phil checks in, showers, and shaves. He sits down and writes some notes on the hotel stationery - he needs to organize his thoughts, to bolster his confidence. He hopes he has not miscalculated by not waiting for an invitation from Leigh Ann. But it is too late for second thoughts. Doubting himself had fucked him royally in the past. He has to see this mission through.

Of course, he has lied to Rosie about what he is doing this weekend. She thinks he is on an overnight ride with Art. Before he goes, he has to touch base with her. She does not answer her phone, so he leaves a message. "Hey, Rose. All is well. The weather was great and we made it just fine. I'm headed out for a few beers and a bite to eat with Art. No need to call back. I'll text you in the morning when we take off. Hug everyone for me. Love you. See you soon." He sets his phone down on the desk. He will leave it here in the hotel, just in case Rosie decides to call him anyway. There will come a time when he can explain it all to her, but he needs to be free of his everyday life, to feel unencumbered by his reality.

An hour later, he is on his bike and heading toward his destination. He passes the campus of the college where Leigh Ann teaches. The late afternoon sun feels good on his face. He tries to take it all in. Everything is in bloom, as it had been when they had last been together. He turns down her street and recognizes the charming old house he had seen on her Facebook page.

He notices a beat up red pick- up truck parked across the street from it. He slows down, pulls into the driveway, and gets off his bike. A black cat and a white cat skitter across the lawn. He takes off his helmet and gloves, reaches into his saddlebag and carefully pulls out the gift. As he walks toward her front door with it, an orange tabby hisses at him from the top step. It launches itself and runs toward the street.

Phil walks up the three steps, turns the crank of the old-fashioned buzzer and then waits on the porch.

Chapter Eleven — Intervention

"Charlotte, what are you thinking? You know I can't let you stay here!"

A few weeks before, Leigh Ann had finally realized that this kid's problems were way beyond her scope of empathy and understanding. That crazy Hamlet essay had been the catalyst, the last straw for her. She had called the Counseling Center as soon as she had finished reading it.

At first she had been surprised to hear her friend Adam Messinger's voice when she had asked to speak to Charlotte's counselor. At the Happy Hour where they had last been together, she had told him that the pest who had been texting her was Charlotte. Although he had made his opinion clear that she should not allow the girl to invade Leigh Ann's personal space, he had not told her that Charlotte was his client. Privacy laws, of course, Leigh Ann had thought in hindsight. He wouldn't have revealed that fact, even to a friend.

She and Adam had been hired by Allegany Community College the same year, and they became fast friends. Throughout their years at the college, they had shared a mutual distaste for each administration that cycled through the institution, as well as for every Republican politician, local state, and national. Adam had originally worked at a college in the Hudson Valley around the same time she had been at Vassar, and like Leigh Ann, he wanted to move back to that area some day. They also had both continued to smoke weed throughout the upper end of their middle age, so there was that too.

A year after Peter had left, Adam told her that he had always thought her husband was a pompous jerk. Adam himself had been divorced years before. Since the break-up of her marriage, Leigh Ann would happily invite Adam as her plus one to events that required it and he could count on her to return the favor.

Because Leigh Ann trusted her friend, she was relieved when it was Adam to whom she turned over the Hamlet essay and subsequently, all of the other emails and text messages she had received from Charlotte. Adam was considered by the college administration to be somewhat of an iconoclast, yes, but he had followed the prescribed protocol in Charlotte's case. Because in her essay the girl had written about suicidal ideation, he had no choice. He immediately made the obligatory referral to the Student Crisis Intervention Team for that reason, but he was also concerned about Charlotte's obsessive need to reach out to Leigh Ann, and that behavior would be a subject for the Team's consideration too. The group included, besides Adam, the dean of students, two faculty members, a consulting psychiatrist, and the college's public safety officer. Leigh Ann was relieved when he told her that the team would most likely not need to hear from her, that the documents she had given him would speak for themselves.

The Student Crisis Intervention Team had convened and made their decision within just a couple of hours. Charlotte received an official dictum from the college: she must withdraw immediately from her English class. From this day forward she would not be permitted to enroll in any of Professor Fray's classes. She would also need to attend weekly counseling sessions until the end of the semester. In June, the team would meet with Adam and the psychiatrist and then the college would make a decision regarding her status for the next year.

After the Intervention Team meeting, Adam, Leigh Ann, and Charlotte had sat together at a small, round table in his cramped office. Leigh Ann had been resistant to the idea, but Adam told her it would give Charlotte an official closure on their relationship. It would be less likely that the girl would be tempted to reach out to her again. "Charlotte, do you understand why the Crisis Intervention Team recommended that you take an Incomplete in your English class this semester?" he asked her.

The girl looked angrily at the Beatles poster over his head and said nothing.

"Professor Fray was right in contacting me. She cares very much about your well-being." Adam's calmness had a soothing effect on Leigh Ann, who had been very anxious about having to face the girl, but Charlotte continued to stare coldly at Sergeant Pepper. "Some of the things you wrote about yourself in your Hamlet essay were very disturbing." He paused for a moment. "As far as your other efforts to communicate with the your professor, the text messages you've sent to her, along with the many phone calls you've been making, could be seen as harassment, which is something the college takes very seriously." The kid finally looked at him directly.

"But, I would never hurt Leigh Ann!" Her harsh voice took up all the space in the tiny room.

"Charlotte, I've made an appointment for you to be seen by Dr. Harris, a psychiatrist who comes to the campus once a week." He lowered his volume even more and said, "As your counselor and the representative of the college, I must do this when a student gives any indication that she might harm herself or someone else." Charlotte resumed her over-his-head stare.

"Can I go now?" she asked.

Adam called Leigh Ann after their conference with Charlotte. He wanted her to seriously consider getting a restraining order if the kid attempted to make any contact with her again. Leigh Ann had not wanted to do that. And she hadn't had to. Since that day, she had seen the girl only once from her office window, walking across the small campus. The texts, phone calls, voice mails, and emails had stopped.

But now, here Charlotte was in her too-small Kwik Fill uniform, standing in Leigh Ann's study, looking desperate. "I'm sorry I didn't call first, but I knew you probably wouldn't answer. Please, let me just hang out here for a little while. My father's girlfriend is the only one home. Bridget. Remember, I told you about her?" She was so out of breath, Leigh Ann was afraid she was going to hyperventilate.

"My dad and Bud had to go out of town to a funeral, so she's watching the younger kids overnight. She hates me! I'm afraid of what might happen if I go home! Please don't make me go home!" She started to cry.

God, how Leigh Ann hated drama! After Peter had left, she had had none. She coveted her quiet house and the lack of conflict in her life now. But Charlotte's sobbing presence was bringing it back. She wasn't going to tolerate it any more. She grabbed her cell phone from off of her desk. She had Adam on speed dial, as he had requested of her after their meeting with Charlotte. Now she pressed 9 and listened anxiously to his message. "Adam, this is Leigh Ann Fray," she said. "Charlotte White is in my house. She is very upset. Would you please call me as soon as you get this message?"

She turned to the girl, who at that moment sounded as though she were choking. "Sit down. Catch

172

your breath, Charlotte. Mr. Messinger will know what to do." She was trying to mimic the calming tone of Adam, even though she was shaken by the sight of Charlotte who had sat down in Leigh Ann's desk chair.

She reluctantly put her hand on the kid's shoulder. She watched as the girl slowed her breathing, in spite of her obvious agitation. "Leigh Ann, I always just wanted the best for you!" she said now. "I'll go. Please just let me change out of my work clothes, and then I'll go!"

Charlotte stood up, and Leigh Ann felt diminished by the girl's size. She had never really been afraid of her, in spite of the fact that Adam suggested that she should be. But in that moment, she felt a sharp shiver of terror. "Yes. Go ahead. Use the powder room. You remember where it is, right? Just off the kitchen." The last thing she wanted was to have her upstairs in one of the bedrooms. She prayed that Adam would call back soon.

Charlotte walked past the photo gallery in the hallway, backpack over her shoulder, and continued into the kitchen. Leigh Ann stood still, listening to the girl's heavy footsteps. She pictured her walking past the big chestnut table and into the small bathroom at the back of the house. As she strained her ears to hear, she realized that a motorcycle had been idling out front throughout the tense exchange with Charlotte.

Later, she would recall that once the engine was shut off, she had heard the unmistakable complaint of one of her cats, more than likely, Spooky. She went to the door to let him in, but before she could, she heard the sound of the old-fashioned buzzer at the front door. Her mind was racing; could it be that Adam had listened to her message and come?

She opened the door. A stranger stood on the porch. In his hands he held a package wrapped in brown paper. She searched his face.

"Hello, Leigh Ann. Can I come in?" he asked.

Chapter Twelve — FREEdonia

Searching the man's face for a clue, she was stumped. She did not know him. He was white haired and handsome, with piercing blue eyes behind tinted, frameless glasses. She continued to scan the stranger's features, and a sudden spark of recognition flashed and then faded. Silently, she ticked off the possibilities. Former colleague? New neighbor? One of her students from long ago?

"It's Phil, Phil Perrero," he said. From across the decades, his eyes locked into hers once again. She involuntarily sucked in her breath. Jesus, he had come. Uninvited. Just as he had that last time.

Her first college Spring Break was coming to an end, and throughout that long, boring week, she had been sleeping in her childhood bedroom, sometimes until noon or beyond. Leigh Ann had not been able to afford the college sponsored bus trip (did she think they were made out of money? her mother had yelled), so her suite mates had gone to Daytona without her. Her dreams this late morning were the kind she had difficulty shaking off for the rest of the day; she was late for a class, she couldn't find the building, the classroom, her books, the paper that was due. The sound of the Super 90 revving under her window had woken her. And now, here he was, on her front porch. Was she still dreaming?

His affectionate grin broke through her bleariness. "Hey babe, can I come in?" She glanced anxiously at the houses across their narrow street as she closed the door. Her parents were at work, thank God, or they would freak out.

"What are you doing here?" The annoyance in her tone surprised them both.

Phil set his backpack on the floor in the foyer. "I missed you. I couldn't wait another week to see you. I want to talk to you about something important, and I didn't want to do it over the phone. Are you mad?" He put his arms around her waist and pulled her close. He really had missed her. From the time he had boarded the bus back to Utica a few days before, he had not stopped thinking of her.

"No. It's just that my parents are pretty uptight about letting a stranger invade their home, especially one who looks like a dirty hippie…" Her poker face cracked

176

into a smile and Phil grabbed her and kissed her again. "I can hear my father now: 'You let that long-hair into our house! And he gave you no forewarning? What, was he brought up in a barn?'" she said, imitating her father's low growl. Phil let her go.

She smiled up at him, but she felt unnerved by his presence. Leigh Ann was not the ironic, liberated young woman she played at college, and she did not want Phil to discover that. But, really, what was he doing here? He was out of context, now that they were off campus and standing in her house in Sidney. Her parents were going to flip out; she would have to convince him to leave before they got home.

Of course she had not told them about her latest boyfriend. Phil was a freak. A genuine freak, totally free to be who he was. Everyone knew him on campus. He was a junior, popular with every group: the Greeks, male and female, jocks, cheerleaders, political activists, musicians and intellectuals. Professors recognized him and called him by his first name. Seniors and even some graduate students, older, cooler students accepted him as one of their own. Leigh Ann always felt dorky and somewhat star-struck in his presence, although they had been seeing one another exclusively for several months.

But her family... how could she subject Phil to her family?

Last summer, as they drove through downtown Toronto on a rare family vacation, her little brother Matt had pointed and stared at young men who looked like Phil. "Hippie! Hippie!" he had shouted out the back window of their big Bonneville, as though he had discovered and was naming some one-of-a-kind species. Leigh Ann elbowed him in the stomach as he boisterously sang the lyrics to that summer's novelty song, "Are you a boy, or are you a girl? You may be a boy, you look like a girl..." Although no one but Leigh Ann and her delighted parents seemed to hear him, she felt a wave of disgust come over her. Her family was embarrassing and idiotic. She was *so* done with them; even her father, whom she loved and respected, was difficult to be around these days. She couldn't wait to go to college in the fall.

To get away from Sidney, New York, would have been her honest answer, had anyone asked her why she wanted to go to college. Like many seventeen year olds of her generation, she had no concrete aspirations. Lucky for her she was enrolling in a state college at a time in history when the Jeffersonian vision of a liberal arts education was still the mission of most institutions of higher learning. The Great Thinker had agreed with the Greek philosophers that any person (any white person, anyway) fortunate enough to live in a democracy should learn and study what was essential to become a free person. He should acquire the ability to read and write; he should study foreign languages, grammar and philosophy, knowledge of which would make for an educated and articulate person. Once that education was mastered, one could then partake as an active and free citizen in that society.

Leigh Ann did not know exactly what liberal arts meant, but had she considered the definition at seventeen, she would have certainly admitted that she *did* want to be free. Yes, she had been a B+ student throughout high school. No, she did not know what she wanted to major in; she could not have told you that summer what her academic interests were, although she loved to read. She, of course, had no idea what she wanted to be when she grew up. Going along to get along, so far, she had free- floated pleasantly through her adolescence. In high school, she had made decisions, academic and otherwise, based upon her friend's choices, but only if those options met with her parents' approval.

Why bother trying to think for herself? Life was just easier if someone else did the planning.

However, that effortless life in Sidney was definitely not her own, and she was growing restless in its confinement. It was possible for her parents to monitor almost every move she made. They had intimate knowledge of Leigh Ann's circle of friends, the boys she dated, her teachers, her employers at her part-time and summer jobs. Both sets of grandparents lived within blocks of their Elm Street home. What her parents didn't witness themselves, they could find out quite easily from their various sources. She was watched closely, and protected lovingly, and until her eighteenth summer, she had been a happy captive. But her parents and her brothers had started to drive her crazy. The small house in the small town was confining and then smothering her; just in time, she made her escape. The State University of New York at Fredonia had set her free.

Fredonia! For Leigh Ann, it was the place where she would finally begin to figure out who she was and what she could become. "FREEEDONIA," students screamed back ecstatically at Groucho during the annual midnight screening of *Duck Soup*, none louder than

Leigh Ann. Unlike that fictional dictatorship in the Marx Brothers movie, her college was democracy in its most ideal form. Fredonia had liberated her from that small town mentality and constant parental scrutiny. At last, she had unlimited options and privacy which the four hundred mile distance from her hometown guaranteed her.

During her first semester, she found it possible to indulge herself in every avenue of exploration that had been shut down in Sidney. By that October, she had taken a leave of absence from Catholicism and its confining doctrine, and was attending B'hai meetings. She discovered music that was far removed from the standard sugary pop fare that she had enjoyed in high school. Cream, Jimmy Hendrix, the Beatles under the influence of Ravi Shankar and the Maharishi, Janis, and funky Motown, but not the Temptations style of Motown, Sly-and-the-Family-Stone- Motown. She partied, partied, partied at college apartments, and downtown bars. Fredonia was a renown music school, with gifted students playing weekend gigs in rock and blues bands for their beer money; for a cover charge of fifty cents, Leigh Ann heard amazing groups and danced into the early mornings. She drank, smoked, and ingested everything that was offered her.

And the friends she was making, so different from the high school classmates she had known since kindergarten. Her suite mates were Long Island girls, so fashionable, so worldly and cool. Leigh Ann was enamored with their accents, and mimicked them whenever she felt the need to sound more sophisticated. She practiced their style of hyperbole too. She chewed gum in a smart-ass fashion, cracking bubbles with her back molars. She consciously extricated the flat vowel sounds that gave away the fact that she was a girl from the backwoods of the Catskills.

She had been trying out her version of a West Islip inflection on a couple of guys from Saint Bonaventure University when she first encountered Phil Perrero. It was the night of The Battle of the Bands held at the County Fairgrounds. A college sponsored annual Beer Blast, it was a Bacchanalian affair and an artifact of the 60's, before society had become so temperate and litigious. For a dollar, students from Fredonia and other campuses from the tri-state area could come and drink, dance, puke, smoke some weed behind the fairground buildings, screw outside in the surrounding woods, and because their hands had been stamped, come back inside and drink some more.

When, years later, Leigh Ann's own kids were students at this same school in the first decade of the 21st century, she joined them for a few hours at Fred Fest, the politically correct grandchild of the Floral Hall Beer Blasts. It was held the weekend before finals started, and it offered an opportunity for kids to relax and chill before they got down to the business of studying for their tests. There was an intramural, mixed gender soccer match. The student government sponsored Frisbee contests, karaoke, beach volleyball, and band competitions. Leigh Ann was there to watch as both her daughter's and son's bands competed for the $100 prize.

She had looked around at the crowd as Lilly's band performed. Leigh Ann would have described this event as good, clean fun, clearly not their mother's beer blast. Some kids were drinking from the standard red plastic cups, but they looked much more clear-minded than she and her peers had been a generation ago in this same college town. Since then, the drinking age had been raised from eighteen. And so many of Lilly's and David's classmates looked perfectly air-brushed and in charge at 21. Their maturity on display even at a party like this one, they made it obvious that for them, college was the place they had to be before their real lives, their money-making lives, could start.

Her own kids were as freaky as they came, in that place, at that time. They were punk musicians, one studying acting, the other philosophy. They had taken their mother's words, "You can be anything you want to be when you grow up," seriously. Leigh Ann had often felt overshadowed by her kids' self-assuredness, even when they were small. What a good job they, she, had done with them.

That November night in 1968, Leigh Ann saw Phil Perrero standing with several other of the college's most popular hippies at one of the makeshift bar tables, livestock feed barrels turned upside down, holding his clear, plastic cup to his eye. He was squinting through this primitive telescope in her direction as she desperately sought a ladies' room.

"Hey, it's back there," he said. Leigh Ann flushed with pleasure at having been noticed by someone as cool as Phil Perrero. She had observed him on campus, seen him in the student union in front of the only television available in those days watching Laugh In on Monday nights, and then again when LBJ announced he would not run. Quite often she found herself watching him as he walked ahead of her, striding from one brick classroom building to another. Now he was smiling at her and pointing to the restroom she had passed. She waved awkwardly and turned back in the direction of the bathroom. When she came back out, there he was standing outside of the door leaning against the wall with a beer in each hand.

Phil's body, long and lean, was nothing like the bulky jocks she had preferred in high school. His hair was longer than hers, flowing wildly down his back. Except for John Lennon, she had never known anyone to wear glasses like his. The thin, rounded wire framed his deep blue, guileless eyes. Always smiling, a faint hint of a dimple flashed from time to time on his left cheek. She had seen his picture and read about him in both the campus newspaper and its underground counterpart. He was a leader in the peace movement on campus, and liberal-minded professors were including him in meetings and protest rallies in Buffalo and the surrounding area. At twenty, Phil radiated confidence. He seemed to know who he was and what he wanted. And that night, to her delight, he made it very clear that he wanted Leigh Ann.

And now here he was in her front hall in Sidney, although he had not told her he was coming. But that was Phil, confident that anything he decided to do was the right thing. It was this self-assuredness that attracted, and at the same time, if she was being honest, intimidated her. He was an only child whose father had left when he was a baby. Maybe that's why he seemed so much more poised than she, comfortable in every situation. He didn't have two parents who watched over him and second-guessed every choice he made.

The night they had seen Hendrix, he had told her he loved her in the backseat of a stranger's car. Who was this girl who would dare to hitchhike hundreds of miles on a school night? More and more, Leigh Ann did not recognize herself when she was with him; when she left his side to go to class or back to her suite, she often felt exhausted, and she had to admit, a little relieved.

Now it was Spring Break and during the past week, she had done little more than indulge her need for sleep. She was back in Sidney, her parents' domain. It had shocked her how quickly she had reverted back to Leigh Ann from high school, Tony and Katy's daughter. Her father would hate Phil, she knew. He had served in the Solomon Islands as a Marine during the war. He disparaged any person, especially a young person, who flew in the face of mainstream conventional wisdom, as Phil most definitely did. Tony Fray would not have to grill him, as he had every other boy she had ever brought to the house. He would see who Phil was, just by looking at him. Her dad was a hard ass, for sure, but Leigh Ann was his favorite child of the three. He had kept her safe from her mother's drunken weekend rants; he had protected her as best he could from Katy's scathing monologues about her only daughter's selfishness. And by God he would keep her safe from this long-haired, army-jacket wearing, Chink-motorcycle-riding Hippie!

Leigh Ann looked over Phil's shoulder at the grandfather clock. In three hours she would have to face her father's angry disappointment and her mother's Seven & Seven fuelled sarcasm. But standing in front of her was the boy who had shown her the thrill of being free. She took him by the hand and led him upstairs to her tiny dormer bedroom. She closed the door behind them, and dropped the needle on the record she had been listening to last night. As she sat down next to Phil on her single bed, Janis Joplin wailed, *Don't you know I been searching/ Oh yes I have/ One good man/ Oh ain't much, honey ain't much/ It's only everything.* He kissed her so gently on the lips, she felt dizzy.

Forty years later, Phil leaned across her threshold and once again kissed her softly. "Well, can I come in?" he asked.

Chapter Thirteen — Glass

Phil experienced a strange resistance, a force almost physical, pushing him backward the moment Leigh Ann opened her door. He wasn't sure what it was-perhaps the fact that she had not recognized him immediately had made him feel this way. He willed himself to place one foot in front of the other as she led him into her home.

A few steps beyond the modest-sized foyer was Leigh Ann's study. His eyes surveyed the inviting room. He knew that inspecting and labeling every object was a necessity, otherwise this dizzying uneasiness would get the better of him. He inhaled deeply and noticed the intense blue color that warmed the walls and the brightly patterned area rugs that covered one- hundred-and-fifty-year-old pine floors. There was a long, oak desk holding piles of papers, books, a laptop and printer. On the wall opposite were two bookshelves loaded floor to ceiling. A pair of cozy red leather chairs were set in front of the stone fireplace, its mantle an antique barn beam. A sound system, including an old pair of huge Dynaco speakers, took up much of the built-in entertainment center on a third wall. A portion of the cabinetry held what looked like hundreds of vinyl albums. Flanking the huge piece were framed posters, the Beatles' Abbey Road cover, young Springsteen at The Stone Pony, a youthful guitar-slinging Dylan walking down a street in the Village. There was a black and white print of children in a 50's classroom; written on the chalkboard, were Zappa's famous words: "Without deviation from the norm, progress is not possible." As he looked toward the narrow hallway that led to the back section of the house, he saw dozens of framed photographs hanging on the walls.

This entire room seemed to be a temple to the time period that they had shared as young lovers. Funky and a little frenetic, so different from the style of the great room in Phil's and Rosie's home. He still loved music, but his primary source of it these days came from cyberspace; he mainly downloaded it from the internet. In the room where he and Rosie spent most of their time, the smallest and most efficient Boze speakers were responsible for the clarity of their listening experience. The Perreros' main living space was modern, with neutral colors on large expanses of mostly bare walls. Chairs from the Art Deco era, researched and purchased at prices well under their worth by Rosie, faced a gas fireplace. Surrounded by cobalt blue glass tiles, the pattern was an original design created and inlayed by Phil. Throughout the years before he had gotten sober, he had hardly noticed the details in the interior of their house. But his wife took Phil's lead when the kids had moved out and they had decided to redecorate. "Clean, like me," he had told his wife, when she asked him what style he would like.

Why was he thinking about home? And Rosie? It and she were what he had settled for after he returned from Nam. He was finally where he was meant to be. This room and this woman were the proof that there had been a golden era in his life, a time of innocence and possibilities. He had come to rediscover her and that time. He had come to find himself again.

The light-headedness had passed. He ended his inventory of the room and turned his discerning gaze upon Leigh Ann. The girl inside the middle-aged woman had to be there, as he had felt she had been through her emails. "Leigh Ann, I hope you're okay with my coming, even though you didn't ask me to," he spoke at last.

She had not moved from the spot in front of her desk the whole time he had been exploring the room. She looked shaken, maybe even a little stunned. "I'm really not sure I'm okay with it, Phil. It's been a very long time." She started a slow pace, back and forth in front of her desk. "Your last email was somewhat disturbing, to tell you the truth. Up until I received that one, it seemed like a wonderful idea, to walk back in time and rediscover who we were, but..."

Phil watched her, spellbound. He could clearly see that the woman was uncomfortable. She seemed to be struggling to find the right words. "Maybe it's been too long to try to go back. We've each lived a lifetime since our days at Fredonia. If you've come here looking for an answer about what happened to us all those years ago..."

A cold dread began to creep up the back of his neck to his scalp. He had to get her off of this path she was on, or it would ruin everything. "I'm sorry I didn't wait for an invitation, but I've been trying hard not to think about you, about us, for a very long time. But then, out of the blue, I ended up in Sidney on that road trip and saw your parents' house." He didn't want her to think he was crazy, although he was beginning to realize perhaps she did. He wanted to be able to clearly express how convinced he was that they were meant to reconnect, that it had been more than coincidence that brought him here today.

"Hey, buddy, it's going to be a beautiful day for a ride," Art had said as Phil answered his phone that early April morning. "What do you say we head for the hills? Tell Rosie you'll be back before the sun sets." Art Malloy worked with Phil. He, too, was a Vietnam vet, so besides loving their fast motorcycles, it would seem that they had a lot in common. But Art had tried just once to talk about Nam back when they had first met, and Phil had shut him down immediately. So work and motorcycles remained the bonding agents between them. Art had been hired at Petit Glass a few months after Phil, and during those first years of getting to know one another, Art had noticed that the guy would go cold and silent every few months. A few times a month Phil would show up on a job site obviously hung over. Art did not judge him. He continued to fight his own demons left over from Nam, but unlike his buddy, Art's nature was to talk about it with anyone who would listen.

For the past couple of months, Phil had been fighting anxiety and depression once again. Art did not know that this phase was different from those other dark days of Phil's that he had witnessed. The lab results on a third biopsy of a mole that had been over his right eye were "ambiguous," his doctor had said. They were sending another specimen to a lab in California, but Phil felt sure in his gut that the death sentence was weeks away. He could not, would not tell his wife or anyone else. As he drove home after work, he struggled to keep driving past the many bars that lined the streets of the industrial zone where Petit Glass was located. Late at night he stopped in front of the liquor cabinet in the great room and contemplated taking just one belt of Jameson. He fought the urge, and as Rosie had requested, he went to a shrink at the VA instead. It was the young doctor who had set him on this path to find out what brought him joy.

"Yeah, let's do it," he had said to Art.

The decision had turned out to be a fateful one. The ride had included sunshine, the temperature, a premature 75 by mid-morning, thrilling hills and curves, and a bonus: unusual April scenery. Frost's "first green" had outlined the landscape in gold this year. Hope, though only a faint glimmer, sparked in Phil as he became part of his machine and this day. Art had mapped out the route without Phil's input; he was glad to just be along for the ride, literally. Two hours into their adventure, Phil saw Art's turn signal flash, and decades after that first trip, he was once again getting off Route 17 at the Sidney exit. They pulled into a diner, and over lunch, the usual taciturn Phil shocked his friend by telling him the story of his first love, a girl who had grown up in this town.

After lunch, he and Art drove down Elm Street. Phil recognized the house immediately, and they pulled their bikes to the curb in front of it. A rush came over Phil. There was a synchronicity to this trip. He hadn't planned it, but the revelation hit him. He was meant to be here today. He almost forgot that Art was with him as the memory of that Spring Break came back to him, crystal-clear.

As Phil and Leigh Ann made love that day, he had become more convinced than ever that they had something incredible, and that he had been right to come. Running through his head were corny song lyrics, implanted in his subconscious by his mother's incessant playing of the 40's ballads she loved. Leigh Ann and he were meant for each other. Their love was here to stay. They belonged together. He needed her by his side for school, his anti-war efforts, for anything to have meaning. He would never find anyone as wonderful as Leigh Ann. She was beautiful, sexy, and smarter than she knew. He believed in her, although he understood that she did not believe in herself. He would help her to gain self-confidence. A deep and overwhelming certainty struck Phil: there's would be a great love and life! He needed to take measures now to bring his vision to fruition. He had to do it right, though. She had told him many times how close she was with her father. And fathers were not familiar territory for Phil. He didn't have one himself, and maybe that's why he had always tried to stay away from his prior girlfriends' dads. Standing in Leigh Ann's study decades later, a father of two daughters himself, he would have to admit that his passionate twenty-year old nature had probably freaked the old man out.

Leigh Ann had stopped pacing and was looking at him now.

"I don't want to upset you, Leigh Ann. Please, believe me," he said. She crossed the room and sat down on one of the chairs in front of the fireplace. He followed, the package still in his hand.

"We shared something so beautiful as kids; there's no one left who knew me, the Phil I was then, like you did. And I knew you, too." Stay calm, keep your voice low, he coached himself.

She shook her head slowly. "In these years since my marriage broke up, I think I've come a long way in understanding myself. But until I *had* to face some hard realities about myself... you thought you knew me?" She shook her head and emitted a low laugh. "I didn't even know me then. I think I was just playing one role or another to suit the occasion or the expectations of other people."

She paused. She looked down at the rug at her feet and seemed to be noticing its pattern for the first time. When she looked back up at his face, she spoke very calmly. "I think you may have wasted time and gasoline if you think I can answer some important questions you may have."

Panic sweat started to form at his brow. He couldn't speak, so instead, he held out the package he had carried in his saddlebag.

"What's this?" she asked.

"A gift. You inspired it."

She took it from him and slowly removed the brown paper. Inside was an object encased in bubble wrap. As she unwound the plastic, Phil saw with relief that the fragile piece was intact. He had created the design prototype a month ago on his computer. As a glazier, he was a master at piecing together the broken designs of other artists, and although he had been making stained glass sun catchers and small lampshades as gifts for several years, he had never produced such a complicated piece before.

The idea had come to him as he awoke in the middle of the night, shortly after he had found Leigh Ann's profile on line. Each night after that, he went to his basement workshop after Rosie and he had eaten dinner. His wife knew he was working on a stained glass piece that she supposed would be a gift for one of his daughters or grandkids, or perhaps even for her. So, as was typical of her, she asked him no questions. Rosie had always respected the spaces, physical and emotional that Phil staked out. It wasn't always easy to do this, but for the past month, she was feeling less burdened by this reserve she must maintain for the sake of their relationship. It seemed as though Phil's most recent gloom had lifted. She silently thanked his new therapist and whatever part of the universe that helped her husband escape his past, however brief the respite might be.

Phil had chosen the colors and types of glass carefully. He already had most of the materials he would need in his workshop, leftovers from earlier projects. The finished piece could not exceed the space he had in his saddlebag, and that limitation cut down on the supplies he would need. He had already scored and snapped each piece of glass perfectly, a step that often frustrated amateurs. The expert cutting of glass required a perfect balance of strength and gentleness, and Phil was a master at this skill. He had measured and cut the lead came for the piece the night before. With his lathakin, he had engraved channels into each piece of the soft metal, so that the separate portions of glass would fit perfectly.

On the job, his favorite part of glass restoration had been the actual glazing, the leading of the pieces.

Most hobbyists ended up having to groze or trim some of the glass components in order for them to fit, but Phil was a professional. Like jigsaw puzzle pieces, the cut glass fit perfectly into the lead grooves. Tonight, he would be soldering. He checked each joint once more. All of them were smooth and snug with no gaps.

When his iron reached the perfect temperature, he put on his safety glasses, and began soldering each lead joint. He loved this part; for Phil, it was the easiest and fastest step in the process. He knew just the right amount of time and the perfect amount of pressure to apply to each joint to melt the lead. When he had finished, all of the margins were smooth and solid, neat and flat. He held the piece up to the light over his workshop table and admired his effort.

"This is so beautiful, Phil," Leigh Ann exclaimed. "You made this?"

"Yes. Not many people have a job that they choose to do as a hobby in their spare time, but I've always loved stained glass."

Leigh Ann could not take her eyes away from his creation. "I love the colors! And there are one, two, three different types of glass here, aren't there?" Her amazed and delighted eyes perused each section.

"Yes, that crimson red piece is over one hundred years old. I took it out of a cathedral window in Albany when my company replaced it."

"Incredible!" Her thrilled smile was genuine.

He had planned on telling her all about it, that his original design was inspired by something he had read in her newspaper column, *Convergences*. He thought he understood the meaning of that word, but just to be positive, he had looked it up. "*A coming together from different directions, especially a uniting or merging of groups that were originally opposed or very different.*"

Her writing had impressed him; he had read several of her essays, but there was one in particular that moved him. It was about a chance encounter she had had when she returned to visit the Hudson Valley, her home before her husband had taken a job in Western New York. At a dinner party, she was seated next to a woman who had been an early colleague in Leigh Ann's first English department. As young women, they had been on the opposite end of the spectrum in so many ways; their teaching styles, their politics, the way they raised their young children. In almost all of their beliefs and the way they conducted themselves, they had been diametrically opposed. Their loud arguments in department meetings followed by months of uncomfortable silences made the rest of their colleagues very nervous. Years later, the hostess on this night had disregarded or simply forgotten the bad blood that had marked their past, and there they were seated next to one another at the dinner party.

At first uncomfortable in each other's close company at the table, they eventually broke through their mutual uneasiness with benign small talk. And then, with no understanding of why she did this, Leigh Ann found herself sharing something that she had not admitted to those around the table whom she had considered her friends: Peter had left her.

The woman who had been her nemesis in a former time dropped the mask of strained cordiality she had worn throughout the evening. She was sincerely sympathetic and with good reason. She confided in Leigh Ann that she had recently and suddenly become a widow, and that very few people knew that a month before he had died, with no warning her husband had moved into an apartment without her. "Leigh Ann," she admitted, "I'm not sure why I'm telling you this. I've kept it pretty much to myself until now."

After that evening, they began to draw on one another for support. They emailed and talked on the phone. As dissimilar as they had seemed in their twenties and thirties, now they each felt a comfort and a genuine empathy from the other. Later in their lives, they had forged a friendship that replaced the passionate enmity that had existed between the two as younger women. *"When a human connection is made unexpectedly, out of nowhere, hope arises; life seems full of possibilities and worth living, even in the darkest times,"* Leigh Ann had written in conclusion.

It was the essence of her closing words that Phil had wanted to depict in his design. The center of the convergence was the point at which his blueprint began. Encased in an opaque circle of deep blue was the pattern that Leigh Ann had noticed decades before on the arm of the freaky guy who owned the head shop in Fredonia's downtown. It was a cold Saturday afternoon in February when the two of them had walked into "The Purple Caterpillar."

"Ooo... I love it," she had said, when the hirsute clerk had rolled up his sleeves and shown her his newest tattoo. It was an elaborate sun, its inner arc mirroring the curve of a half moon. "Did you know," she asked

Phil, "that in almost all cultures, the sun is male and the moon is female? I love the way they are separate and connected at the same time in this design," she had said.

Phil's creation was catching the waning light from the study window as Leigh Ann held it up in front of her. The two overlaid triangles formed a star; its six points each held an alternating pattern of a single sun, rays bursting from the orb, and the three moons, each in a different stage: waxing, waning, and full. The centerpiece was made from translucent glass, the sun a canary yellow and the half moon a pearly cerulean blue. Phil had used a bubbled white commercial glass as the background for the main motif. The three solitary moons on the tips of the stars were an opaque, pale blue. The single suns were made from the same yellow piece as the central sun, but these smaller orbs lacked its curvy black rays. Phil had carefully scored these from a piece of transparent glass. The design was intricate, and both the leading and the cut of the glass were exceptional.

"Absolutely incredible!" Leigh Ann said.

Although he could see she was delighted with his gift, Phil was struggling to shake off that feeling, an alienation that was growing. On the ride here, he thought about how he would explain his design to her. He would say that he had read her columns and that he realized that she believed in the power of fate and coincidence. That people could connect again, no matter where their lives had taken them, or perhaps because of that. This stained glass piece was his interpretation of that philosophy, his Convergence.

He had planned on asking her, 'Do you see how the whole piece is connected through that center moon and sun? The single stages and phases lead right back to those conjoined figures." He would tell her that he believed in unintended consequences. That their young love and her abandoning it and him had set a chain reaction in motion, one which had devastated him. And now that he had found her again, he needed to know why she had changed her mind about marrying him. He wanted to open his mouth and speak, but he found that he could say nothing.

As young lovers, they held each other that April afternoon, warm from the sex, young and in love. "Leigh Ann," he said, "Will you marry me?"

He did not expect her nervous laughter. "Sure. How about we wait until we're old enough to buy a drink in Pennsylvania?" He got up out of her bed and pulled his jeans on.

"No, I'm serious. I don't want to be without you. After this semester, let's get married. They're building those new married student apartments on Brigham Road. I'll call and put a deposit on one for the fall." He pulled on his T-shirt. She realized he was using the same tone he used when he was dominating a discussion in one of his classes. She would be standing outside the door waiting for him and she could hear his confident voice. He began pacing around her bedroom, just as she had seen him do when he spoke at organizational meetings and peace rallies,

"Phil. I don't know what to say. Yes, I guess? But my parents are definitely going to be upset! They have no idea..." her voice trailed off as she sat up and looked at her alarm clock. "They're going to be home from work any minute."

"Don't worry. I'm going to have a meeting with Tony Fray tonight."

"Oh God..." she uttered as though she were praying.

"I'll ask him for your hand, and I'll give him every reason why being married will make us better students, better people. You've always said he's a by-the-book guy, but a reasonable one too." He reached for her one more time and tried to reassure her with a kiss.

After a silent dinner eaten at the Fray's kitchen table, Tony had listened, stone-faced, as Phil sat across from him in their small den. He refused to let that the old man's cold stare inhibit him. He laid out the plan, logically, convincingly, Phil had assured himself. After a long silence, interrupted only by the grandfather clock's bonging, Tony Fray stood up and said, "Better get some sleep." With a slight jerk of his head he indicated the tiny sofa. "You've got a long ride home in the morning."

For rest of the night and that next morning, Phil had waited anxiously for her, but Leigh Ann had not come down from her room. He could have never guessed that she was through with him, that from this day forward, they would lead separate lives.

"There is a bay window in front of the breakfast nook in my kitchen looking out on the garden," she said now. "That's just where this beautiful piece belongs." She stood up and said, "How about a beer or a glass of wine? I could use some Pinot right now."

"Just coffee, if you have it," he answered as he followed her into the narrow hallway. Phil stopped in front of the framed photographs. Leigh Ann came back and stood next to him.

The first pictures he looked at were from a time and place familiar to him. He might have been posing next to Leigh Ann in some of them, if his life had not gone down a path that took him thousands of miles away to a hostile jungle. There was a blurry picture of some guy standing behind her with his arms wrapped around her waist. They stood in front of a stage with hundreds of other fans, a fuzzy, but recognizable, guitarist mid-riff in the background. "Is that Hendrix?" he asked her.

"Yes. I saw him a second time at Woodstock. My dad threw me out of the house that summer for defying him and going, but it was definitely worth it." So she *could* stand up to her father back then, if she wanted something badly enough. He looked at her, but she seemed unaware of the irony of her answer.

Here was a twenty- year- old Leigh Ann, mid-shout among dozens of other students in front of Phil's freshman dorm building. In her hand, a homemade sign, the letters bright red, "On strike! We're going to shut it down!" He had read about the National Guard killing those Kent State students from his hospital bed in Hawaii. A friend from Fredonia had written to him around that same time, ecstatic that SUNY students too, had forced the hand of the governor; the campus was closed, and they would not have to take finals this semester! At the time, Phil could not appreciate the pain of those whose kids were being gunned down, nor the immature happiness of his friend. He was in serious withdrawal from heroin and still in the throes of his Vietnam experience.

The last black and white photo on the wall was Leigh Ann in cap and gown squinting into the sun in front of Fenton Hall, the English building. She seemed to be glowing with pride in the picture and in this moment, as well. He turned to her and she smiled at him. She was obviously happy that he had stopped and looked at this gallery of her life.

He turned his eyes to a remarkable collage. Leigh Ann in a group of people posing with Robert Kennedy. "A friend and I went to one of his rallies in New York City," she explained. The next one was Leigh Ann and several other women standing with Bill and Hillary. "I saw them at Chautauqua when he was the governor of Arkansas," she said. The third photo was a much clearer night shot of Leigh Ann in a throng at Grant Park, the new First Family on the platform behind her, beaming. "I had a conference in Chicago the week before the election. I took my chances that he was going to win and stayed a couple of days longer."

On the wall closer to the connecting dining room were dozens of pictures of friends and relatives, all strangers to Phil. The last section on this wall was dedicated to her travels. The young, middle-aged, and then older Leigh Ann, in Mykonos, Delphi, Sicily, Florence, Venice, Paris, Amsterdam, Macchu Picchu.

She pointed to the wall behind them. "My heart," she said, indicating the dozens of pictures of her son and daughter, from infants to young adults. The display spanned this entire wall. The most current images were framed posters of their respective bands. As Leigh Ann joyfully narrated the stories of her kids' lives, she was unaware that the man next to her was somewhere else. Somewhere she had never been, farther away than any of her travels had taken her.

M-16 in hand, he stepped warily inside what he prayed was an abandoned hut. His nightlight searched for evidence that people had lived here only hours before. What they had left behind, Phil surveyed as though he were reading a book. The center of the hut was used for drying rice and bamboo; everything else was ancillary. Five straw mattresses lay on the floor in one corner of the open room. Nearby, articles of clothing and two hats were scattered on the floor. Across from the beds on a crudely fashioned low table, stood four bowls of noodles with three pairs of chopsticks, one of them child-sized. On the perimeter were two crude bamboo chairs and one small table made of rattan. Phil shone his light on something he saw lying on it. He picked up a piece of paper with an illustration and recognized it as one of the dozens of leaflets the US Army distributed to the peasants. He could not read the captions written in the dialect of this region, but in cartoonish depictions he saw soldiers building houses, distributing food to smiling peasants, and administering medicine to infants. He put the paper down. Next to the leaflet were several Polaroid pictures. He picked them up and studied each one. A wedding picture; the bride and groom, who could have not been more than fifteen, looked stoically back at him. Another showed an elderly lady holding a baby, both of them dressed in silk robes and formally posed. There were three more pictures of people who appeared to be dead, their eyes closed, Phil assumed, forever. A dead young woman, old man, and a baby. Strangers who were haunting him even now.

He looked at the woman standing closer to him than she had in forty years. Her eyes radiated love as they scanned the images of her kids' faces. A sickening wave of something suddenly came over him. It was the same sensation he had felt as he lay on his cot in the jungle following a night raid. He would awaken in the dead of the night, and whatever it was would engulf him, a suffocating vapor. He felt alienated, displaced, and at the same time a desperation and a longing that was physical overwhelmed him. He begged his lungs to take in oxygen and prayed for his heart to beat. When it happened in Nam, he had not wanted to analyze it or name it. He just wanted it to go away. Now, as he stood next to Leigh Ann after all these years, he understood what it was. He had been, and was now, homesick.

"Come on," she said cheerfully, as she walked on toward the back of her house. She cautiously carried the stained glass piece. "I'll make some coffee; I want to hang this beautiful glass in my window."

She was totally unaware of Phil's apprehension. He was feeling once again, as he had in Vietnam, that he was invading the privacy of a stranger.

This had been a mistake, he told himself.

She had lived a lifetime without him. He wouldn't ask her the question. She did not know him and she could not save him after all.

Chapter Fourteen — Convergence

Phil followed Leigh Ann as she walked toward her kitchen. As he did, he had the sensation that he was slogging through thick mud. "Could you hold this, please?" she asked him, as she carefully handed back his gift.

She needed both hands to push open the heavy oak door that separated the dining room from the kitchen, and he watched as she bent down and propped it open with the wooden wedge that served as a doorstop. He noticed for the first time that she was bare-footed, as she must have been since he had arrived. She led him over the threshold into the fading light of the kitchen and reached out to take the stained glass piece from him. Cautiously, she set it down on the counter of the large center island.

Phil was trying to come to terms with the overwhelming sense of loss that was threatening to drown him. He turned away from her as she walked toward the coffee maker, obviously unaware of his angst. Leigh Ann had not stopped smiling since recounting for Phil the highlights of her children's lives.

The sunset framed by the kitchen window was a pink and red springtime anomaly for Western New York. The bay window could not be original to the old house, his expert's eye told him. Phil moved across the room to get a closer look. A beautiful chestnut table, the kind found in early twentieth century farmhouses, stood in front of it. In the center of the table was a ceramic planter. A white orchid, foreign to this cold place, bloomed within.

Phil's crushing disappointment suddenly gave way to clarity, to a revelation. Standing here in her home, in her presence, he realized that he had placed too much value on the significance of his relationship with Leigh Ann. It was not her abandonment of him that had led him to live a dishonest life. Had the realization come too late? As he stared at the flower, the urge to escape the house overwhelmed him. He started to feel panicky, as though he was being confined against his will. He saw that a narrow hallway led to a back door out to the yard. "Do you mind if I check out your the garden?" he asked as he turned back toward Leigh Ann.

"Of course not," she said as she began to grind the coffee beans. She stopped a moment and said, "When it gets dark enough, I'll turn on the little white lights I've strung in the trees."

Phil headed in the direction of the doorway to the garden. Maybe he would give Rose another call while he was out there. He knew how worried his wife had been about him. Just last week, she had brought up the subject of their taking a trip together. "Back to Nam," she had said gently. Things had changed drastically in the decades since his deployment, she said. She had read that a lot of vets who took the journey back found it a positive and healing experience. The thought of hearing his wife's voice lifted his spirits. He would call her. Shit! He had left his phone at the hotel. At least he would walk outside and catch his breath. Then, he would have his coffee and go back to the hotel. He would call Rosie and…

Suddenly, he was overwhelmed by a psychic sense, a warning flash, similar to the ones he had experienced in the bush as a young infantryman. An orange blur darted out from the dark hallway. He did not have time to wonder why the Kwik Fill girl was here. Charlotte pointed the .38 at Phil's abdomen, where the Voice had told her it would do the most damage.

The coffee grinder muted the first shot. He heard the second pop before he'd felt anything. He fell backward onto the slate floor. At first, the pain was like a machete in his gut. Then he felt an incredible burning, like boiling water was being poured onto his internal organs. The noise of the grinder stopped.

"Charlotte!" Leigh Ann did not move, frozen by the shocking sight of this girl in her kitchen. She knew in that instant, she was bereft of the inviolability of her home forever. She had the sensation that she sometimes had, when in the midst of a dream, she realized it was about to turn into a nightmare. "Oh, Jesus, Phil!" she screamed as she looked down. She ran toward his collapsed body and dropped to her knees beside him. Blood had splattered all over the lower kitchen cabinets, several feet from where he lay. She grabbed the dishtowel from the oven door and pressed it as firmly as she dared against his lower abdomen.

"Oh my God! Phil, Phil can you hear me? Open your eyes, look at me!" she pleaded. Phil heard her voice from far away. He could not answer.

"Jesus Christ, Charlotte! What did you do?"
Still clutching the gun, the girl moved closer to where
Leigh Ann knelt over him.

Charlotte listened as the Voice buzzed and
droned inside her head. "Leigh Ann, this man is the evil
I warned you about! He was going to trick you and take
you with him! I had to stop him! I have to keep you
safe!" she said.

As the girl ranted, Leigh Ann continued to bear
down on Phil's wound. The small towel had become
soaked with his blood. Her hands were covered with it.
Within seconds, the cuffs of her white sweater were
drenched too.

"We are going away, Leigh Ann..." Charlotte's
hands trembled as she pointed the gun at the two of them
on the floor. "We can go to California or Oregon where
David and Lilly are! We'll start a new life together..."
she realized she was shouting. *Calm down*, the Voice
warned her.

Leigh Ann dropped the saturated towel and
scrambled to her feet. Charlotte's words did not register
with her as real. This man who lay bleeding on her floor
was proof enough that the girl was violent, but Leigh
Ann was certain that Charlotte would not shoot her. She

had to get help for Phil. Where was her phone? Maybe on her desk. The same sort of adrenaline rush she had felt years before when she had protected David from his father was emboldening her now. She began to run through the dining room to the study, heedless of Charlotte's screaming behind her, "Don't do it Leigh Ann! I'll kill you and then myself! I swear, I will!"

Phil was alone. He placed his right hand on his gut, the place where at least one of the bullets must have entered. He opened his right eye and brought his hand up to it. Blood. As a young boy, the sight of it had made his knees go weak. But now... he had seen so much blood in Nam... so much mud and blood. He turned his head to the side and watched the thin red stream flowing through the gray grout line of the slate tiles. More than anything, he did not want to lose consciousness. He concentrated on the fluid rivulet of his blood. Old floors, slanted, he thought.

Even though his gut burned from the acid his organs were releasing, his whole body was freezing. The pain intensified as each moment passed, but he willed himself to stay awake. He knew he could not survive this, but as that realization washed over him, so did a strange calm. During his time in Vietnam he had witnessed how death would sometimes wait, even for those who did not look like they had a chance of stalling it. The day that Lieutenant Netti had done just that was what Phil thought about now as he lay bleeding on the floor of this alien place.

Phil and his team had been walking through the jungle on an unusual daytime assignment. They had been joined by another squad from their platoon led by a lieutenant called CMF, Crazy Mother Fucker, so dubbed by the men he commanded. His given name was Jack Netti, but he had rightfully earned the nickname. His hot temper was legendary on the Fire Base. When he was pissed, and he was pissed often, he would rant and rave and kick anything that was in his path. On that day he was upset about having been rousted out of his cot after only three hours of sleep. The platoon was being sent through the jungle on foot to the small hamlet they had torched twelve hours before. From the air, suspicious activity had been reported, and their mission on this morning was to make sure that absolutely no VC had survived the night attack.

As they marched through the dense foliage to a mucky path, Netti kept up his angry protest to Phil's sergeant. "I tell you Dietrich, I'm sick of it! Every goddamned time a monkey makes a move in the trees, these goddamned copter guys, with their heads up their asses, think they spot Viet Cong." He was spitting and sputtering now. "And which lackeys do they send into the bush to do the dirty work?" If there had been something to pound his fists on, Netti would have done just that.

A few yards ahead of them, an object in the mud caught Phil's eye. It looked like braided strips of bamboo, and as they got closer, he could see it was a crudely made doll. A fleeing child had probably dropped it as her family ran to escape whichever force wanted them out of their homes. Netti saw it too. "I tell you Dietrich, I cannot wait to get out of this hellhole!" He punctuated every word with a fuming stomp as he headed toward it.

"Lieutenant! No!" Dietrich screamed, just as Netti's foot, with an angry kick, made contact with the doll.

Phil watched as a leg flew up in the air and came to a rest against a tree, yards from where the land mine had gone off. He turned away, sickened, and looked back to the spot where the doll had been. In its place was a human head and neck attached to a torso. The bomb had transformed Lieutenant Netti into a half-man. A river of blood flowed on the jungle path in front of them. The two medics scrambled to administer morphine, and as the injections entered his bloodstream, that son of a bitch, no longer truly among the living, did something Phil and everyone present that day would never forget.

Jack Netti started to laugh his ass off.

The ubiquitous birdcalls and buzzing insect noises of the jungle were drowned out by his raucous laughter. For a full five minutes, the horrified platoon stood transfixed as Corporal Netti's ghost laughed.

If Netti could steal those five minutes from Death, could laugh in its face, Phil knew he could do the same. He ran his hands down his thighs. His jeans were soaked with blood, but his legs were still attached, and he might be able to stand for as long as he would need. He reached for the cabinet closest to him and pulled himself up to the counter. As he stood, he struggled to keep his eyes opened and focused. In front of him, where Leigh Ann had laid it, was his stained glass piece, his Convergence.

"I will work and I won't ask you for anything! I will protect you from harm always. Leigh Ann, you need me!" He listened to the crazy girl's voice coming from somewhere in the front of the house.

"Let go of my goddamned phone, Charlotte!" Leigh Ann shouted. He heard a scuffle, objects dropping on hardwood, then footsteps and the girl's hysterical voice coming closer.

"No! Stop! Please listen to me Leigh Ann!" Her voice was shrill and wilder than it had been.

He heard Leigh Ann, unshaken, insistent. "Charlotte, we're not going anywhere together! You need help!" What was Leigh Ann doing? he wondered. Could she not see that this psycho had every intention of killing her too? In spite of his pain, in that moment, he marveled at her courage.

Phil leaned heavily on the cabinet for leverage. The glazier knew the spot where, with just the right amount of pressure, he could achieve the most effective fracture. He picked up the glass and smashed it against the countertop. A moment of silence followed the sound that could be made only by shattering glass. And then the shouting voice of the crazy girl came closer.

"Leigh Ann! Stop! I mean it! Don't go back in there! I'll shoot you and then me..." Charlotte watched as Leigh Ann disappeared through the kitchen doorway.

Since she had shot the man, she felt the light and warmth that was Leigh Ann retreating, moving very far away from her.

Charlotte had been resisting The Voice's command: *You failed to execute the plan, Charlotte. Shoot Leigh Ann and then yourself.* The girl knew that there were two bullets left in the chamber of the .38. And more rounds in her backpack. She would give Leigh Ann one more chance to change her mind; if she did not, Charlotte would do what the Voice demanded.

Charlotte, seconds behind Leigh Ann, ran to the kitchen. She was almost panting, trying to catch her breath as she crossed the threshold. She had not noticed that the door was now only three-quarters of the way open. The wooden wedge had been moved a few inches forward.

Leigh Ann stood facing the girl, holding tightly to the kitchen island, pale but resolute. Charlotte stared for a moment at the face of the woman that she loved. Then she pointed her father's old revolver and cocked the hammer back. "Leigh Ann, please, please, don't make me do this." She glanced down to that place on the floor where Phil had fallen. She saw broken pieces of colored glass in a pool of blood, and to Charlotte's horror, nothing else. "Where..."

Leigh Ann watched in astonishment as Phil stepped out from behind the heavy oak door, the weapon in his hand. She wanted to shout, to warn the girl, but her vocal chords were frozen. She could not believe that this nightmare was happening. She wondered how long these two people, strangers to one another, had been on a path to this day. To her house. To her.

In the instant that Charlotte had crossed the kitchen threshold and cocked the .38, Phil recalled what he had committed to memory so many years ago. The words of a Revolutionary War major that appeared on the cover of the Army Rangers Manual: "Let the enemy come till he's almost close enough to touch. Then let him have it, and jump out and finish him with your hatchet."

The image of a striking snake flashed in Leigh Ann's mind as Phil grabbed Charlotte from behind and pulled her by her hair so that she was looking up at the ceiling. The girl had lost sight of Leigh Ann. "Drop the gun," Phil said. Empowered by The Voice, which was everywhere now, the girl would not let it go. In spite of being bent backwards in a kind of macabre yoga pose, she screamed and struggled to free herself from his dead man's grip. And as the Voice cheered her on, Charlotte pulled the trigger.

In a weird state of detachment, Phil put aside his revulsion for the violence and the horrors of his days in Nam. Now, when he needed to, he was operating on the autopilot of the combat soldier; the instructional diagrams of the most effective techniques to employ during hand-to-hand combat seemed to be right there in front of him. Swiftly, deftly, he sliced through the screaming girl's jugular with the broken glass. Still, she screamed. At the first cut, a buzzing sound accompanied her shrieks. The air escaping her windpipe sounded like the whistle of a teakettle, but still she screamed. The revolver fell from her hand, cracking a slate tile.

Her mouth remained wide opened in a final, silent scream. Phil pushed the large body away from him. Charlotte fell to the floor, her arms and legs twitching. Phil released his weapon from his grasp, and the sun and moon shattered on the slate next to her.

Phil slumped backward against the broad oak door and slid in slow motion to the floor. Leigh Ann had been transfixed by the horror she had witnessed;

now she moved automatically toward him. She stepped over Charlotte's body. She was aware of the slipperiness of the blood on her bare feet as she went to Phil. She lay down beside him and put her arms around him. "You are very brave," she heard him whisper.

But Leigh Ann knew the truth. She had always been a coward, and today she had had a reckoning. She had faced the horrible consequences of her inaction.

"Leigh Ann," he groaned, "it hurts so much..."

As soon as he spoke those words, Leigh Ann had a vision, so vivid, perhaps it was a hallucination. She desperately wished Phil could see it too, to feel the power of the epiphany that she was experiencing. She saw two young lovers lying on the bed in Sidney. As the girl held the boy, she said to him, "I'm only eighteen, you are just twenty. We have our whole lives ahead of us."

Four decades too late, she finally had the wisdom and the courage to tell him the truth as she had known it since the moment he had proposed. He was the first boy she had loved, but she was just beginning to know herself, and so she could not promise to love him forever. She would tell him that now.

But Phil spoke instead. "I told you it would be a hard time for both of us," he said.

Chapter Fifteen — Post-Mortem

Leigh Ann could not judge how long it had been since Adam Messinger had found her lying on the floor of her kitchen, covered in blood, her arms around the waist of a dead man. She hadn't heard him come into the house, but in a dream, he had called out to her from another room. She tried, but she could not respond. The next thing she was aware of was his voice again, but now he seemed to be in the room with her. Was he talking to himself? "Yes. I'd like to report a crime. My name is Adam Messinger. I am at the home of a friend. Her name is Leigh Ann Fray. She is a professor at the college. Her address is 20 West Terrace. Yes, in the city. Yes, Allegany. There are two gravely injured people here; they may be dead. One was shot, yes, I see the firearm. There is blood everywhere. No, not my friend. She's alive. Yes, I know one of them. She's a student. Was. Her name is Charlotte White. There is a man too. He is the one who was shot. I don't know him. Yes, thank you."

The rest of the night's events were hazy and disjointed. At some point, Adam had helped her to disentangle herself from the lifeless man. He pulled her up so she could stand, and he put his arm around her shoulder as he led her into the study.

When the front buzzer sounded, he opened the door. Leigh Ann recognized one of the two patrolmen as soon as Adam let them in. He was a former student, Paul something, she didn't hear him say what his last name was and she was too fuzzy headed to recall it. He was discrete and courteous as he surveyed the study and took pictures of the room and then of Leigh Ann with a digital camera. " Emergency Services will arrive soon, Dr. Fray," he told her. She was feeling light-headed and Adam guided her to one of the leather chairs. He pulled the second one closer to her and sat, holding on to her hand.

The other officer was looking around the room and writing in a notepad. "Dr. Fray, I need to ask you some questions about the deceased and what happened here today." It took her only a few minutes to sum up what she knew.

Officer Paul opened the door to the three EMT's. He led two of them into the kitchen. The third person, a woman, stayed in the study. She set a plastic case on Leigh Ann's desk, opened it and started pulling items out of it. Was she speaking to Adam or her, Leigh Ann wondered. Her words made no sense. Something about vitals and shock. She sat on the leather chair while the woman poked and prodded her. She watched as she attached a clip to Leigh Ann's index finger, took it off, put it back on. She wrapped a cuff around her bicep and pushed the pump until it had reached a maximum constriction. Several times she put a cold stethoscope to her chest and back. Then she was applying something wet to each of her feet. Leigh Ann realized she was speaking to her. "Did you step on broken glass?' she asked.

"Maybe," she answered. Tweezers of some sort were pulled out of the case.

"Yes, you did," the woman said, showing her the first of dozens of tiny red slivers she had just retrieved. Again, cold moisture on her feet as the woman cleaned her small wounds. She pulled bandages out of the case and applied them.

Throughout this bizarre routine, Leigh Ann was trying hard to concentrate on the footsteps of the policemen and the other EMT's as they walked around the bodies in her kitchen. "What do you think they're doing?" she asked Adam.

"I'm not sure, Leigh. Taking more pictures, probably," he said. She felt sorry for the cops and the ES people. When was the last time there had been a murder, never mind two, in Allegany? She knew in her gut that they would have to arrest her. Somehow she had caused this horror.

The two patrolmen came into the study. "How are you doing, Dr. Fray?" officer Paul asked her, sounding genuinely concerned. She had always insisted that her students call her by her first name. The proper-sounding "Dr.", she thought, caused a barrier that might impede their involvement in learning. She was sure the young cop had called her Leigh Ann when he had been her student. This formality was a sign of her new status. She was responsible for two deaths, and because of this, she would be called by her official title.

The EMT seemed to be speaking for Leigh Ann. "Dr. Fray initially was showing symptoms of compensated shock. When we first arrived, her pulse rate was elevated and I could detect a mild tachycardia. Her skin was cold and clammy and she seemed confused when we first arrived. Her vitals have all stabilized over the course of the last thirty minutes, however. She also suffered some minor lacerations on the bottoms of both feet. I cleaned and dressed them."

"Thanks, Dina," the patrolman said. "Dr. Fray, the Forensics Team will be here in a half-hour. They'll need your permission to look at your computer and your phone records, since you told the other officer that they contain some communication you had with both the victim and the suspect. The Crime Lab people and the coroner will be spending the better part of the night in your house, gathering evidence. I've talked with my supervisor and he says it would be alright if you stay somewhere else for the night, as long as it's in the city. You might be able to get some sleep if you did."

She looked at Adam who was nodding in agreement. "Can she change out of those clothes first?" he asked the officer.

"Of course. Just put them in this bag for the Forensics Team," he said to her. "Dina, why don't you go with her?"

Dried blood had stiffened her jeans. She pulled them off along with her sweater and handed them to the EMT. After she dressed, Dina stood by her as she packed an overnight bag.

"Just give me an address and a phone number where you can be reached," the patrolman said as she came down the stairs. "Detective Taddio wants to meet with you tomorrow at the station at two."

Together she and Adam walked out past Phil's motorcycle, still parked in her driveway, into the mild spring night. He had asked her to stay at his house, but she had said no. She needed to be alone. They drove along the river to the Marriot in stunned silence. "I'll call you in the morning," he told her.

The clerk at the desk was the only person she saw as she checked in. She took the stairs to the sixth floor, avoiding the elevator and other people. She dropped her bag on the bed, undressed, and stood under the hot water in the shower for a half an hour.

She put on pajamas, and crossed the room to open the drapes. The lights from the ski resorts in Ellicottville cast an artificial brightness across the valley. She sat down in the easy chair, a piece of furniture supplied to give a home-away-from-home impression. Leigh Ann stared out the window at the city and towns below and wondered how in the hell she had ended up here.

Chapter Sixteen — Q & A

Detective Chuck Taddio, sleeves rolled up and carrying two cups of coffee from Tim Horton's, walked back into the small interview room of the Allegany Police Department. Last night, after the coroner's official pronouncement, the officers on duty had tracked down the names and addresses of the next-of-kin of both the suspect and the victim. By 7 AM, Taddio had made the necessary phone calls.

Since then, he had spent the majority of this Sunday studying emails, texts, and the documents from the college's Crisis Intervention Team. He had interviewed Adam Messinger, who had been succinctly informative. For the last two hours, Taddio had been questioning Leigh Ann Fray.

He had left her alone for a while with copies of Phil Perrero's emails and the piece of stationery they had found in his hotel room. Leigh Ann was sitting at the small round table in the center of the room, and for the third time she was reading the notes Phil had jotted

down yesterday before coming to her house. Taddio set
the cups down on the table, saying nothing, and stood
over her, watching as she read.

Allegany Marriot
Allegany, New York

Questions:
- Why did you stop loving me?
- Why did you let your father tell me that you didn't want me there?
- At school, why did you act like I was dead to you?

Everything changed for me then

Nam
- Saw things that were wrong
- Should have stopped them
- Couldn't
- Have felt guilty ever since
- Guilt doesn't let me feel much else

I do love my wife.
Would never leave her.

Why I'm Here:
- When we were together, I was proud of who I was
- Felt I could do/be anything

- Want to remember and feel like that again - can you help me remember what that was like?
- Feel like I was meant to find you again, (convergence!) that there is something to be gained, maybe for both of us

Cancer is back

This last line had been crossed out.

Leigh Ann stopped reading and looked up at the detective. Taddio slid one of the cups of coffee in front of her and sat down, facing the professor. She had admitted to him that she had not slept at all last night. Women her age did not look well when sleep deprived, he thought to himself. Although she was an attractive woman, the video play-back of the interview would not be flattering.

"So, Dr. Fray, we've talked for awhile about what happened in your home yesterday. We're trying now to figure out *why* it happened. Why do you think Mr. Perrero traveled across the state yesterday to see you?"

"All I know is what's right here in his emails and these notes. It seems that he thought I could help him recover something he'd lost when we broke up all those years ago," she said.

"When you received his first email, what did you think about his trying to find you again?" The detective was unrolling his shirtsleeves, and then methodically folding them back up to his elbows.

"I was flattered at first, but after I wrote back and received his third message, I didn't think it was a good idea to invite him. I didn't really remember clearly what had happened when we were young, why I had broken it off with him. I didn't know what his questions for me would be, or what he was looking to get from me. And he made it clear that he was married." Her eyes fell on the notes he had made on the stationery.

"So after that third email, you never invited him to come for a visit, right? "

"No. I was actually planning on writing to him yesterday. To tell him I didn't want to see him. But I didn't get the chance."

"And how did you feel when he showed up at your door yesterday?" the detective asked.

"Shocked. Put off."

"Put off? What do you mean?"

"When he first got there, I felt like he was invading my privacy."

He looked directly at her. "But you let him stay." It was a statement, not a question.

"Well, I couldn't throw him out after he had come all that way. And as we talked, I could see that he was a nice person, that he intended me no harm. He didn't put me on the spot," she said.

"So you didn't ask this man, who you hadn't seen in forty years, who was really a stranger to you, you didn't ask him to leave?"

"No."

"And then he became a murder victim and a hero, all in one day." It seemed to Leigh Ann that this was not a question for her, but a closing to the speech the detective had just delivered. He took a sip of his coffee.

"Yes," she said anyway.

"What a shame, huh?"

"Yes," she said.

"Okay, Dr. Fray. Now I'd like to talk with you about your relationship with the suspect, Charlotte White, alright?" On the table in front of him was a manila folder. He opened it.

"Yes," she answered.

"When did you first meet Charlotte?" The detective shuffled through several sheets of paper as he questioned her.

"She enrolled in my Developmental class two years ago."

"Developmental. Is that a remedial class of some kind?"

"Not exactly. It's more of a preparatory program for students who need extra support, especially in writing skills, so that they can succeed in college. The classes are smaller than the typical composition or lit classes. There are more opportunities for one-on-one assistance and conferencing." The detective could hear that she was struggling to frame her answer in layman's terms.

Now he looked up from the papers and stared directly at her. "And how did Charlotte do, with all of this extra attention?"

"What do you mean?" The afternoon sun was coming in through the small window at the top of the wall she faced. She held her hand up to her eyes to shield them.

"Did she become a good college student?"

"No. I wouldn't say so. She struggled to get C's, in English classes, anyway." Leigh Ann wrapped both hands around the coffee cup, eager for its warmth. In spite of the sun on her face, it felt like the AC was running full blast in the tiny room.

Taddio shuffled more papers and then his eyes began to scan the document in front of him. "And how many of your classes did she take in all?" he asked.

"She had completed three. She had been taking my Writing About Literature class this past semester too, but she withdrew after the findings of the Crisis Intervention Team."

He looked up at the teacher. "Is that typical? For a student to take that many courses from the same instructor?" he asked in his flattest voice. He did not want to give away any clue as to what his gut had been telling him.

"No. It's not typical. We are a small department on a small campus, so if a student wants to go on to a BA in English, he might end up with the same instructor in several courses in that area, but that was not the case with Charlotte." She took the lid off of the coffee cup, hands shaking. Steam rose, but she was not deterred. She did not sip; she gulped.

He looked down at the paper. "Yeah. I can see by her transcripts that she wasn't heading in any clear direction academically." He raised his eyes to hers and asked, "So why do you think she took all of those classes with you?"

The professor dropped her eyes. Silence.

"She told me she felt safe in my classroom." Leigh Ann emitted an almost imperceptible sob when she said the word "safe." Her eyes were watery when they met his. "Sorry," she whispered.

"That's okay." He slid the box of tissues across the table. "You've been through a lot." The detective had been impressed with the woman's composure throughout these hours of questioning. He had left it up to Paul Davies, the patrolman who had been on the scene last night, to make the call to postpone the detective's interview until today. To Davies, who had known her as a teacher, she had seemed confused, and the ES staff had confirmed that she was in a mild state of shock.

Taddio silently counted to ten and said, "Did you ever meet with Charlotte outside of the classroom?"

"Yes. In my office. She would frequently drop in without an appointment. Students will sometimes do that." Leigh Ann finished dabbing her eyes with the tissue.

"But Charlotte did this more often than these other students who dropped in on you, right?"

"Yes."

"And when she surprised you in your office like this, how long would she stay?"

"She didn't have a vehicle and she had to depend on her brother to get her home after classes. So she sometimes would stay in my office for hours. She knew what my teaching schedule was..." Taddio's eyes widened. "It's posted outside of my office. That's standard procedure at the college." She continued her explanation. "So unless I wanted to go home or hang out in the Faculty Lounge... It was difficult to get her to leave. It was easier to let her stay." Her voice trailed off at the last part of her explanation.

"Did it occur to you that this might be a problem? These frequent visits to your office?" Taddio's even tone belied his hunch, that the professor knew just how sick this kid was, and exactly how intently she was fixated on Leigh Ann.

"No." She sat up straighter and squared her shoulders as she faced him again. "I just thought that she was a lonely kid. No rules were being broken, Detective Taddio. I've had students throughout the many years that I have taught that have wanted to make a connection with someone, anyone. And I believe that what Charlotte saw in me was a sympathetic adult." Her attitude had changed to an almost authoritarian insistence.

"And did these other lonely students call your cell phone, your home phone, your office phone, and leave dozens of messages? Did they send you hundreds of texts? It actually took me a number of hours to read them all, Dr. Fray. Do your students usually text you?" He wasn't quite matching the certainty of her tone, but he wanted her to know that he meant business.

"No." Leigh Ann dropped her eyes to the table. She picked up the coffee cup. "Charlotte was not well liked by her peers. Her home life was miserable. I guess she felt that I was the only one she could talk to. So I let her talk. It got to the point that I rarely read the texts or listened to her messages, and eventually I just ignored them. It seemed harmless at the time..."

Detective Taddio interrupted her. "So until the essay that you shared with the counseling center, you didn't see any signs that Charlotte was a danger to herself or others?"

Leigh Ann shook her head. "My God, no. I never felt threatened by her," she said with a finality in her voice.

"And what was she like in class, with her peers?" he asked.

"Disliked, for the most part. She had a very abrasive personality in the classroom."

"Was she ever angry in your class?"

Her surprise at this question was evident, as if she wondered how he knew. "Yes. Sometimes when she would get very passionate about something, she would raise her voice during discussions. There would be a lot of eye rolling behind her, for sure. But she was never a threatening presence. Her agitation was annoying, yes, but she never seemed angry enough to do harm to anyone." Leigh Ann looked directly into the detective's eyes.

"But there did come a time when you called on the Student Counseling Center, when you thought that she might harm herself, correct?"

"Yes. She had written a disturbing essay, the one you have there, " She looked toward the folder.

"And then the College Crisis Intervention Team convened to determine if Miss White had the potential to do harm to herself and perhaps to others, right?"

"Yes."

"And in their discussions, they were concerned with the obsessive behavior she displayed regarding you, correct?"

"Yes."

"And didn't the Team mandate that she withdraw from your class? And Adam Messinger, Charlotte's counselor, also recommended that you get a restraining order against her, correct?"

"Yes..."

Again, he cut her off. "But you didn't, correct?" He didn't wait for her to answer. "Why not?" He wanted the truth about this relationship, so he had speeded up the pace of his questioning.

The professor dropped her head again. "I didn't see the need. The kid had a rough enough time of it. I thought she was harmless. To others, anyway."

"I see. So you didn't bother to get a restraining order. Dr. Fray, at the beginning of our interview this morning, you stated that Charlotte had come to your house several times before yesterday, that previous to submitting that Hamlet essay, she had actually stayed overnight in your home." Now he was looking at her like she was a slide under his microscope.

"Yes. During a blizzard. She lives... lived in Hinsdale. She didn't have a vehicle or a license, as I've explained. She couldn't get home and she asked if she could stay at my place. Detective, she had nowhere else to go," Leigh Ann insisted.

"Do you have a car, Dr. Fray?" he asked. He did not give her a chance to answer.

"There are three bedrooms in your home, correct?" Again, he didn't wait for a response. "Which one did she sleep in that night? And where did you sleep?"

"Yes, there are three. I slept upstairs in my room and I made up the couch in the study on the first floor for her." For the first time, Taddio recognized a sheepishness in her voice. "I think she may have found the book of passwords that I keep on my desk in that room. After I had gone to sleep."

"And you believe on that night she may have read the emails exchanged by you and Mr. Perrero?"

"Yes."

"Did you ever talk with Ms. White about Mr. Pererro?"

"No! Of course not! My relationship with Charlotte went one way. I never involved her in my personal life!"

"And yet she knew you were divorced. Charlotte knew the addresses of your children. She knew where you lived, as a matter of fact, she had slept overnight in your home, Dr. Fray. She had your cell number and your computer passwords. She knew that Mr. Perrero was interested in rekindling a relationship with you..."

"Yes, that's all true, but..."

His next questions came in even more rapid-fire succession. "And, Dr. Fray, you've told me that after Charlotte shot this man in your kitchen, as he lay on the floor bleeding, she held a gun on you and shared her plan for your life together, correct?"

"Yes."

"And when you resisted her at this point, she threatened your life and her suicide, right?"

"Yes."

"But you and Charlotte were nothing more than teacher and student, right?"

Leigh Ann had paled. She seemed physically incapable of answering him.

Taddio leaned in toward her and asked, "How did Charlotte White manage to hide in your home yesterday? How was she able to get inside and ambush and kill Mr. Perrero?"

She could not speak.

And in the midst of this silence, Chuck Taddio realized that his suspicion had been wrong. A jealousy infused lover *was* to blame for Phil Perrero's death. But the object of Charlotte's affection, this intelligent, successful woman sitting in front of him had buried her head in the sand. She had ignored all the danger signals that Charlotte had given her. She had had no idea that the troubled girl had been in love with her.

"I let her in," Leigh Ann Fray finally managed to answer.

Chapter Seventeen — Hamartia

CONVERGENCES

Final Words
by Leigh Ann Fray

I have been living in and writing from a small cottage located on my daughter's property in Portland. She resides in the "main house" adjacent to this small bungalow. The former owner of the place was a painter, and this was her studio space. I have been staying here for the past six months. There are three modest-sized rooms, just enough space to contain me and to keep my mind from wandering. I have broken my habit of always having a television on or a stereo playing music as the background sound of my days and nights. It is very quiet here.

This is the place where I have come to try to regain my footing after the tragedy that took place in my Allegany home. Writing this column has often been a therapeutic undertaking for me. I hope my readers will indulge me, one last time, as I attempt to analyze and gain insight from a most horrific event.

Most of you who are reading this column are Western New Yorkers, or part-time residents of the region. If so, you are probably already familiar with the details of the two deaths that occurred in my home last May. The police and the coroner have submitted their final reports, and the newspaper and television journalists have shared their accounts. Some of the media have gone beyond the facts and have turned to speculation as to the circumstances and motives of the three people involved. As the only survivor, I have felt it necessary to begin my own investigation, a painful, subjective search, one that I am sure I will never fully finalize. I have had to ask myself many questions: How did this atrocity evolve? What part did I play in the bloody encounter of two strangers that day? What responsibility do I bear for their untimely deaths? Was I the third victim of this tragedy or its catalyst?

As a college English major and then as a professor of literature, I have spent thousands of hours deconstructing the natures and motives of fictional characters. It is no wonder, then, that my method of exploration in a personal calamity is much like that critical approach I have been trained to apply to literary works. A close and thorough reading of a piece of literature is not a simple matter of following the plot. An astute and sensitive reader must notice the subtleties that the author provides in the creation of a character, not only in their interactions with others, but by looking closely at the forces or circumstances that may make them act in a certain way, or change them entirely.

I know that Phil and Charlotte are not characters in a novel or a play; they are two people who are gone from this world too soon. They can't tell their stories in first person accounts. I bear a responsibility to tell what I have come to understand about each of them and how their experiences impacted them. For the past six months, I have attempted to "read" and "reread" not only *their* words and actions, but through painful introspection, my *own* character and accountability in this tragedy. With the permission of each of their families, I have decided to publish in this last column the essence of my discoveries.

Charlotte White was my student, one of thousands I have taught over four decades. Throughout our association, she gave many warning signs of her mental illness. Her delusion, one which I did little to actively discourage, was that I played a more intimate role in her life than just her college English teacher. In hindsight, I can see why she might have come to this misperception. Charlotte was an abandoned child, searching for a mother. When I was confronted with her attempts to become closer to me, I looked away. I took the path of least resistance. She was a troubled girl and she had crossed many boundaries in our two-year association; because it was easier not to confront her, I permitted it. I refused to admit how sick she was until it was too late. By then, she had gained access to my computer passwords and read all of my personal correspondences, including those between an old boyfriend and me, and she had made a plan to stop him from coming back into my life.

Phil Perrero was a man on a life quest the day he came to my door. He wanted to understand the event that, in his mind, had changed his destiny. Although he never had the chance to ask the question directly, I have good reason to believe that he traveled to my home that day to ask me why, forty years before, I had suddenly ended our college love affair. I had accepted his proposal of marriage, and then turned my back on him and pretended that he did not exist. It very well may have been that our break-up influenced his decision, as a twenty year old, to join the army during wartime. According to his family, those demons he encountered while on his tour of duty in Vietnam never left him. His effort to see me after all those years was more than likely an attempt to see through my eyes the innocence and idealism he possessed before his military service. To have me bear witness to that rediscovery of his earlier, happier self.

I have tried numerous times to understand my motivation back then. I was an eighteen-year-old college freshman, trying desperately to develop my own sense of who I was. Phil's passion and self-confidence overpowered me, that I do remember, but I did not possess the maturity or courage to tell him that directly. I did not have the intestinal fortitude to say that it was not only my parents' disapproval of him that ended our relationship. So, I let my father do the dirty work, and I simply went back to my life on campus, relieved when I did not see Phil after that second semester. As with Charlotte, I took the path of least resistance, and though it was a circuitous route, it seems to have lead to a horrible end in my kitchen six months ago.

Phil's wife and I have spent many hours on the phone over these past months, and she is a wise woman; it is no wonder he loved her so much, a fact he confirmed in something he wrote hours before he died. Although she knew nothing of his plan to reconnect with me, she had encouraged him to do what many veterans of the Vietnam War have done: return to the country that seemed to have stripped him of his optimism and hope. She tells me that she would have gladly gone with him on that journey, had he decided to take it. He would never share the exact details of his experience there, but he did tell her that he had discovered the truth about himself during those terrible three months: he was a coward. But Rose Perrero knew the truth about her husband; she saw his strength and valor in their day-to-day lives. After his death, she received letters of condolences from men who had served alongside him in Vietnam. More than one wrote that Phil, because of his unwavering morality, was the bravest man in their unit. I know that Rose and his comrades are right about him. Phil's heroism is the reason that I am alive today.

The ancient Greek dramatists coined the term for a flaw in a character that brings about a downfall. It is *hamartia*. In this tragedy that I lived through, I am culpable. I understand now that it was my disingenuousness that brought the three of us together that night in my kitchen. My passivity contributed to the disaster that took place. I certainly do bear a responsibility for those deaths.

Instead of looking away, I should have paid full attention to the troubling signs Charlotte had been giving throughout our two year association. I should have said, "I am your teacher, not your friend or your mother. I'll show you how you can get the help you need to stand on your own."

If Phil had asked me directly that day, "What happened all those years ago?" that brave man deserved to hear the truth as I had never told it.

That I had not figured out who I was yet. That I had not been ready to get married.

What if I had been authentic and truthful with Charlotte and Phil? Would they both be alive today?

My daughter encourages me to stop thinking about the mistakes I have made. She tells me that it is possible to reinvent oneself. Stay in the present, she says, and in each moment be entirely honest with yourself. Then, you can be fully honest with everyone. At age 58, I am attempting to adopt this new way of living. This last *Convergences* column is my first step in that direction.

Over the years I have used this space to explore the tricks and treats of coincidence and fate. I've concluded in many of these essays that we are hapless wanderers on this path of life and that in fateful moments, when we least expect them, convergences with others from another path can take place. I have written about the happiness or sadness that these junctures can bring. But what I've ignored is the role that free will can play in the course of our lives and the lives of those who we meet along the way. I have missed that crucial truth, and two people have paid the ultimate price for my ignorance. I share this lesson now with you, readers, and hope you will apply it to your own lives, before it is too late.

About the Author

Deborah Madar was born in Buffalo and has been a
Chautauqua County, New York resident for most of her
life. She taught high school and college English for 26
years. She and her husband Gary live in Bemus Point.
The author spent the long, cold winter of 2014 putting
the finishing touches on *Convergence*, her first novel.

Made in the USA
Middletown, DE
16 November 2021

52242394R00146